# "Don't tell me I have to teach you how to kiss, as well as how to flirt?" she murmured invitingly

Luke was breathing harshly. "What's to teach? A kiss is just a kiss...."

She laughed. "Oh, Luke, do you have a *lot* to learn...."

Her condescending mockery was smothered by his urgent mouth. His lips slanted across hers, his tongue smoothing inside the velvety interior of her mouth, sucking at the sweetness he found there. Rosalind's eyes fluttered shut, unable to cope with the sensual overload.

Finally he broke away. "Well, teacher, I guess you made your point."

"Did I?" It was Rosalind who had learned a lesson....s

*Susan Napier brings us yet another fast-paced, witty, breathtakingly sensuous romance that will captivate you till the very last page!*

*SUSAN NAPIER* was born on St. Valentine's Day, so it's not surprising she has developed an enduring love of romantic stories. She started her writing career as a journalist in Auckland, New Zealand, trying her hand at romance fiction only after she had married her handsome boss! Numerous books later she still lives with her most enduring hero, two future heroes—her sons!—two cats and a computer. When she's not writing she likes to read and cook, often simultaneously!

## Books by Susan Napier

**HARLEQUIN PRESENTS**

1554—SECRET ADMIRER
1595—WINTER OF DREAMS
1674—THE CRUELLEST LIE
1707—PHANTOM LOVER
1744—SAVAGE COURTSHIP
1788—THE SISTER SWAP
1847—RECKLESS CONDUCT

# SUSAN NAPIER

## A Lesson in Seduction

**Harlequin Books**

TORONTO • NEW YORK • LONDON
AMSTERDAM • PARIS • SYDNEY • HAMBURG
STOCKHOLM • ATHENS • TOKYO • MILAN
MADRID • WARSAW • BUDAPEST • AUCKLAND

ISBN 0-373-11870-8

A LESSON IN SEDUCTION

First North American Publication 1997.

# CHAPTER ONE

'LEAVE the *country*?'

Rosalind Marlow stopped pacing up and down the hearth-rug in her parents' elegant lounge and stared at her mother in consternation.

'Just for a little while, darling,' Constance Marlow murmured placidly, finishing her cup of tea and settling back on the couch, looking quite unruffled by her daughter's outraged expression. 'Until some of this dreadful fuss dies down.'

'Are you suggesting I *run away*?' Rosalind demanded incredulously, her slender body stiffening in rejection of the idea of such rank cowardice. She and her five siblings had been brought up on the credo that one must always face up to one's responsibilities, no matter how painful or embarrassing. Surely her mother wasn't now suggesting that she compromise her honour for the sake of simple expediency?

Rosalind looked to her father to share her outrage, but he merely gave an expressive shrug, as if to say he was but putty in her mother's hands. Which, of course, he was... but only when it suited him. As a distinguished director with over thirty years' stage experience Michael Marlow was gifted with an unerring ability to control the volatile personalities of the egocentric actors and actresses who cluttered his professional and personal life—his famous wife included.

'Think of it as taking a timely holiday, darling,' her mother murmured in her beautifully articulated drawl. 'You must admit it's absolutely ages since you had a proper one. And after what you went through on that last job you certainly deserve a relaxing break.'

Rosalind shuddered at the memory of her recent, depressing foray into film. The disaster-plagued production had merely served to confirm her inner conviction that, like her mother, she was born for the stage rather than the screen. She liked to think of herself as versatile enough to tackle anything but she had never really enjoyed the disjointed, repetitive nature of acting for the camera, where everything was done in short snatches and some nameless editor in a booth somewhere controlled your ultimate interpretation of a role.

She should never have allowed herself to be flattered into accepting the female lead in the art-house production but the director, an old drama-school friend, had caught her at a weak moment and persuaded her that it would be 'fun' to work together again.

Some fun. Rosalind had cracked a wrist doing her own stunts and had almost been eaten by sharks!

'That's not the point,' she argued, raking her fingers through her short-cropped red hair, making it stand fierily on end, a vibrant contrast to her pale skin and black roll-necked sweater. 'It's the principle of the thing. Why should I let myself be driven into exile, for goodness' sake? I haven't done anything *wrong*!'

'Of course you haven't, darling,' her mother soothed, looking hurt at the implication that she didn't trust her own daughter.

Rosalind simmered with frustration. She knew that her mother was playing shamelessly on her sense of guilt but she had made a promise and not even for her family's peace of mind was she prepared to break it. However, she couldn't blame those she loved for trying to winkle out the truth.

'Even if you had, you know you'd have our unqualified support,' commented her father quietly, making her feel even worse.

'I'd tell you if I could,' she burst out. 'You'll just have to accept my word that I haven't done anything to be ashamed of!'

Her eyes avoided the coffee-table, which was strewn with tabloids bearing lurid headlines that variously branded her as a promiscuous sex-kitten, a butch, feminist home-wrecker, a pathetic, mixed-up waif with an insatiable craving for the love denied her by her disapproving family, and a helpless tool of an alien conspiracy to topple the governments of earth!

'I thought we'd already agreed on that,' murmured her eldest brother from the window-seat, turning his broad back on the entertaining sight of his wife trying to keep up with their three aggressively active toddlers in the rambling back garden of the large town house. Hugh pinned Rosalind with his thoughtful gaze. 'But unfortunately the Press aren't quite so trusting. By refusing to answer questions, you've left them free to speculate without the hindrance of having to conform to the known facts.'

Rosalind scowled, her thick, dark-dyed eyebrows drawing sharply together. 'I gave them a statement; that should have been enough. You're a lawyer; can't I take out an injunction or something, to stop them harassing me?'

She slouched with unconscious grace over to the front window and peeked through the curtains. Sure enough, the gaggle of reporters who had been tailing her relentlessly for the last week was still clustered around the gate. Her wide mouth firmed. She was damned if she was going to allow them to hound her into giving them what they wanted.

At least they were no longer knocking on the door and shouting questions through the keyhole, thanks to Hugh's threats to have them arrested for trespass. His hefty size and cold grey stare had added to the deterrent and not for the first time Roz had blessed her parents for having the lucky foresight to adopt a child who had developed into such an impressive specimen of adult masculinity. The natural Marlow offspring were all tall and slender, more accustomed to using charm than muscle to extricate themselves from trouble.

Hugh shrugged his massive shoulders. 'Possibly, although even if successful all a court order would do would keep reporters at a certain physical distance; it wouldn't stop them digging around for information or photographing you in public. In fact it would probably be counter-productive—make the Press even *more* tenacious. They could counter-claim that the public interest in this case transcends your need for personal privacy because of the political implications—'

'But what happened had nothing to *do* with politics!' Roz wailed, infuriated by the unfairness of it all.

'A politician's wife is involved; that makes it political,' Hugh corrected her with his precise, pedantic logic. 'With an important by-election coming up, all sides are going to be quick to try and use the publicity to their advantage, and while I don't doubt that the Government is as keen as you are to see the story die a discreet death it certainly can't be seen to be interfering with the freedom of the Press.'

'Well, I don't see how my running away is going to help,' said Roz, her green eyes sparkling with ire. 'People are sure to think it's because I'm guilty of *some*thing.'

'So what? They think that anyway,' came another unwelcome brotherly opinion. Sprawled full-length on the floor beside the couch, Richard was genially fending off an assault by two miniature versions of himself.

'Look, Roz, take it from one who knows—all this hide-and-seek is merely whetting the Press's appetite and if you won't oblige them with a scandal they'll create their own. You're God's gift to the tabloid industry, you know: a well-known actress with a reputation for wild behaviour and a sexy body that photographs like a dream. All they have to do if the story threatens to lose impetus is to snap another shot of you in a skimpy dress getting in or out of a cab or threatening to deck another reporter and—presto—instant page three! They love chasing you around . . . you give such good press.'

'Mind your tongue in front of the children, Richard,' his mother chided, rapping him sharply on one up-raised knee.

He grinned irrepressibly, looking much younger than his thirty-one years. He dragged himself up to a sitting position, gently wrestling his sons off his chest. 'Face it, Roz, they're not going to just give up and go away, not while you're dangling yourself tantalisingly under their noses. It's going to get a lot worse before it gets better and the rest of us are bound to suffer along with you.'

His sweeping gesture took in the various members of the Marlow clan who had arrived for what Rosalind had been led to believe was a quiet afternoon tea with her parents. Instead she had found the house bulging with her siblings and their partners and offspring. In fact, the only ones missing from the council of war were her rock-composer brother, Steve, who was currently in Hollywood working on a film score, and her youngest brother, Charlie, who was a mechanic with a race-team on the overseas rally circuit.

For the most part Rosalind was grateful that she came from a close-knit family with a strong interest in each other's well-being, but sometimes their loving inter-ference only complicated matters. Right now she didn't need the extra pressure that they were bringing to bear on her battered self-confidence.

The trouble was that her family still saw her as the over-impulsive, fun-loving and, OK, outright reckless creature that she had been in her teens. Why couldn't they accept her as the mature, capable, staunchly in-dependent twenty-seven-year-old woman she had become? Granted, her basic personality hadn't changed; she was still outgoing and gregarious, throwing herself wholeheartedly into everything she did, and some people might mistake her passionate enjoyment of life for recklessness, but her family should know better.

In the last five years the disciplines and rewards of her profession had become the major focus of her prodigious energies. Because her loyalty, once given, was rarely withdrawn she still had some wild and loose-living friends, but it had been years since she herself had had to be rescued from the consequences of her own folly.

She glanced over to the corner where Olivia sat with her husband, Jordan Pendragon.

Normally she could rely on having her twin firmly on her side, but today Olivia seemed oddly reserved. Like Richard and Steve, Rosalind and Olivia were only fraternal twins, but they had always been closely attuned to each other's emotional wavelength. Olivia's marriage the previous year hadn't seemed to jeopardise their closeness and thus it was disconcerting for Rosalind suddenly to discover herself deprived of the psychic support she had always taken for granted.

Olivia's dreamy, abstracted air was nothing new—as an artist she frequently went around with her head in the clouds—but Rosalind had the feeling that this time the mental aloofness was deliberate, and it hurt. Everything around her seemed to be shifting, changing, veering dangerously out of her control. It was no wonder her nerves were a riot.

'I'm sorry, I had no idea that this was going to turn out to be such a mess,' she sighed, thrusting her hands into the pockets of her skin-tight jeans, her slender shoulders hunching under the thin black sweater. 'The whole thing's been blown up way out of proportion... all because some greedy hotel employee took it into his head to sell his distorted version of events to the highest bidder!' she said bitterly. 'Why can't people mind their own business?'

'People figure that since you make your living in public you *are* their business,' said Richard unsympathetically. 'You're not the only one under siege. My office phone line is tied up handling the constant press calls and I'm fed up with granting interviews that turn out to be a total waste of time...not to mention having to hire security guards to keep reporters away from my cast and crew.'

'I thought you believed that all publicity is good publicity,' said Roz, with a pointed look from Richard to his wife which reminded him of the way he had flagrantly used the gossip columns to manipulate Joanna into accepting his proposal.

'When it's about me, yes,' Richard said deadpan, and with outrageous immodesty, making Joanna put a hand across her mouth to stifle her laughter. 'But they're only gatecrashing my set to ask about *you*...why haven't I cast you in one of my films? Is it because I think you're unstable? Do you have drug/alcohol/attitude problems...what kind of breakfast cereal did you eat as a kid? I tell you, it's driving me nuts! I'm running behind on my shooting schedule as it is; the last thing I need is any more disruptions on the set.

'Do you know we actually filmed five takes of a scene yesterday before I discovered that one of the dead bodies was a reporter from the *Clarion* who had bribed one of the extras to let him take his place? The idiot kept breathing and blinking. Apart from not being able to act, he wasn't even a member of Equity. He could have got me in trouble with the union, for God's sake!'

Of course, she might have known that Richard was more concerned about his precious movie being completed on time than her problems! Rosalind glared at him as he unsuccessfully tried to detach the two red-headed babies from his now woefully stretched woollen jumper.

'Now, Sean, stop sucking Daddy's sweater; you'll get fur balls,' he scolded. 'You too, David; you don't *have* to do everything your brother does...'

As usual his twin sons ignored his stern command and continued to gum the soggy wool, until their mother gently uttered a word and they began to crawl obediently in her direction. Richard watched them go with a rueful smile that acknowledged a higher domestic authority. He scrambled to his feet, wincing slightly at the pressure on his lame knee, and turned his attention back to Rosalind.

'If you genuinely want to deflect press interest the simple solution is to remove yourself as a potential source of information. Disappear completely for a while... at least until the initial feeding frenzy is over. It's not as if you have to worry about walking out on your job,' he added with cheerful malice, 'since you don't happen to have one at the moment...'

'I'm currently resting between engagements,' Rosalind informed him loftily. It was a point of pride that she had hardly been out of steady work since she had left drama school. 'I'm considering several offers—it's just a matter of deciding which one to accept.'

'But you said yourself that none of them start for a few weeks, darling.' Her mother pounced. 'So why not make the most of your free time until then? Your father and I know the *perfect* place for you to go—peaceful, warm, exotic and—best of all as far as you're concerned—wonderfully remote.'

'It's not an island, is it?' said Rosalind with deep suspicion. 'I think I've had enough of remote islands for one lifetime.'

The film she had just completed was supposedly set in just such an idyllic-sounding location. However, the cast and crew had found themselves virtually camping out on an extremely rugged dot in the South Pacific, in wretchedly primitive conditions and beset by all manner of hardships, including erratic delivery of supplies, a subtropical cyclone and Rosalind's terrifyingly close encounter with a shark while filming the underwater scenes.

Needless to say, the budget had been horrendously overrun, and Rosalind had been relieved to get back to New Zealand with body and soul intact, only to walk slap-bang into a situation of almost equal peril.

'Oh, you'll love this one,' her mother assured her. 'Your father and I had one of our honeymoons there a few years ago. We simply *adored* it. A jewel of a place. Gorgeous scenery, gorgeous weather. A perfect refuge from reality.'

'And exactly where is this perfect jewel?' asked Rosalind morosely, unwillingly tempted.

'Tioman Island!' announced her mother with a vocal flourish that invited applause.

She must have forgotten that geography had always been Rosalind's worst subject at school.

'Is it somewhere around the Great Barrier Reef?' she guessed, thinking that if she *had* wanted to wimp out and hide from her avalanching problems Australia would hardly be far enough!

Joanna, the teacher, looked pained. 'It's in the South China Sea,' she said helpfully.

'Oh, right...' Rosalind closed her eyes as she tried to visualise Asia in her head, but her overtaxed brain refused to co-operate. All she could see against the blackness were wretched images from Room 405 at the Harbour Point Hotel in Wellington... Peggy Staines's anguished, pleading face, her body writhing in pain on the crumpled double bed, the frantic actions of the ambulance crew and the avid curiosity of the hotel staff and guests who had seen Rosalind in her bathrobe dazedly gathering up the scattered banknotes from the floor.

'Off the east coast of Malaysia, north-east of Singapore.' Her father gently reorientated her.

'You *must* have heard of it, darling!' her mother urged. 'It's quite famous. They shot parts of *South Pacific* there. Remember Bali Ha'i... remember the waterfall? That was filmed on Tioman. Just imagine being able to visit it for yourself...'

Rosalind's eyes flew open. She loved vintage musical movies. She had a good singing voice and had appeared on stage in a number of musical productions, *South Pacific* included. She vividly remembered the waterfall scene from the movie and her interest quickened, much against her will.

'If it's famous then it's probably packed to the gills with tourists,' she said stubbornly. 'I hate tourist traps.'

'Funny how I couldn't drag you away from Disneyland when you came and stayed with me in LA,' murmured Richard, who had lived and worked in the film capital for several years before he'd turned from acting to directing.

Rosalind poked her tongue out at him. 'Disneyland's different.'

'So is Tioman,' her mother said hurriedly, before sibling raillery could subvert the conversation. 'There are a few resorts but the island's still pretty much uncommercialised, and the pace of life is very slow. There's no stress, there's no crime...it's somewhere you can feel wonderfully safe and anonymous. Even a free spirit like you, Roz, wouldn't feel hemmed in. You really need to see it to appreciate it. I think I just happen to have some brochures around here somewhere... Now where did I put them...? Michael, do you see them?'

She looked around vaguely, absently retucking a loose strand of red hair into her elegant French twist. Rosalind watched suspiciously as her father obediently took his cue and 'discovered' the large stack of travel folders conveniently on hand under one of the newspapers on the coffee-table.

Her suspicions were strengthened by the flagrant enthusiasm with which everyone fell on the glossy brochures. Alluring descriptions of virgin rainforest and white coral beaches were read aloud with typical Marlow panache, the delights of scuba-diving in limpid tropical waters and the merits of Malaysian cuisine discussed. Even the babies drooled in ecstasy over the bright, colourful pamphlets that Richard thrust into their pudgy fingers, although that was probably more to do with the fact that they were teething!

'It says here that there are references to Tioman in Arabic literature that date back two thousand years...' murmured Hugh, perusing a hard-back book that had a stamp on the cover indicating that it had come from the library. Something else her mother had just happened to have on hand? Rosalind didn't think so!

'You know, you don't even need a visa to visit Malaysia,' said Olivia, reading the fine print on the back of a brochure. 'Your passport's current, isn't it, Roz?'

'Of course it is. Roz is used to travelling light. She can take off at the drop of a hat, can't you, darling?' her mother encouraged.

Rosalind thought it was time to put her foot down and inject some reality into the situation.

'Even if I *was* thinking about taking a trip, if this place is so wonderful there's no way there'd be vacancies for spur-of-the-moment travellers,' she said firmly. 'And flights up to the East have wait-lists for their wait-lists. Anyway, I haven't budgeted for any extravagances this month...'

Although Rosalind had inherited a considerable trust fund several years ago, she preferred to live mostly off her own earnings. Large amounts of money made her uneasy. She had no head for figures and small amounts slipped far too easily through her fingers for her to trust herself with serious sums.

Besides, the theatre had a strong historical tradition of poverty amongst its acolytes and it went against the grain to flaunt her unearned prosperity when most of her fellow actors were eking out their meagre pay cheques in a noble state of self-sacrifice for their art. So apart from the occasional rush of blood to the head Rosalind lived a life of cheerful self-sufficiency, content in the knowledge that when she was too old and decrepit to tread the boards she would be able to retire in dignity and comfort.

'Credit me with a little forethought, darling,' said her notoriously disorganised mother. 'As soon as I realised you might need a quiet little bolt-hole I got Jordan to use some of his family's muscle. He still has pull in the Pendragon Corporation and he's made all the arrangements for you through their travel section. Of course the economy flights were overbooked but you're going first class all the way, and don't look like that—you don't have to worry about the cost—I booked everything on your father's credit card...even on Tioman you only have to sign for your accommodation and meals.

'Look, here are all your tickets and documentation. All you have to do is turn up at the airport the day after tomorrow and you'll be on your way to three weeks of carefree bliss.'

Rosalind accepted the proffered blue travel folder numbly, opening it as gingerly as if it were a potential bomb. 'You've already *booked* for me to go?' she said shakily, leafing through the evidence, her eyes widening at the sums involved. She didn't know whether to feel pleased or insulted by her parents' generosity. 'What do you expect me to say?'

Her mother smiled warmly and jumped up to give her a hug. 'No need for thanks, darling. We know how determined you are to stand on your own two feet, but at times like this the family should pull together...'

Rosalind struggled free of the fond maternal embrace. 'Pull together?' she snorted, waving the tickets under her mother's elegant nose. 'You're *bribing* me to go thousands of miles away!'

'We thought it would be a nice early birthday present,' her father ventured.

'My birthday isn't for seven months!' Rosalind pointed out sardonically.

'A *very* early birthday present,' Constance Marlow said, giving her husband a repressive look that told him not to deviate from the script.

She shrewdly studied her daughter's sullen expression and abruptly changed her tactics. She threw up her hands in disgust and said crisply, 'Oh, for goodness' sake, Roz. Talk about people blowing things out of proportion! Stop behaving as if you think we're trying to sweep a blot on the family escutcheon under the carpet.'

She ignored the disrespectful snickers of her offspring at the atrociously mixed metaphor and continued with steely emphasis, 'We're very *proud* to have you as our daughter; we just don't want to see you hurt unnecessarily. And it *is* so unnecessary, darling, what you're putting yourself through. Unless you *like* playing the helpless martyr, of course—then I suppose there's nothing more to be said. I might say that most children would be *delighted* if their parents offered to send them on an all-expenses-paid holiday...'

'I know I would,' said Richard with a languishing sigh.

'I see the Met Office predicts a cold front this weekend,' said Michael Marlow, apropos of nothing. 'They say winter is going to arrive with a vengeance.'

'Tioman does look wonderfully lush and Gauguin-ish,' said Olivia traitorously, her soft, rain-washed green eyes wistful, her smile tinged with strain.

It struck Rosalind that it was her twin who looked as if she needed a holiday, and it was on the tip of her tongue to say so. She glanced at Jordan and found him watching his wife with a narrow-eyed concern that stilled the words in her throat. She felt a flutter of inexplicable panic and her fingers tightened on the tickets in her hand.

'You know, you should make the most of your freedom while you can, Roz,' advised Joanna, rescuing a soggy rusk from the carpet. 'Once you have children, taking a holiday is like going on military manoeuvres.'

As if on command, Hugh's three pre-schoolers came thundering into the room, their diminutive blonde mother breathless in their wake.

'Oh, you are going to Tioman, then? Good on you!' Julia panted, seeing the folder in Rosalind's hand. 'I told Hugh you'd do it, even if only to cock a snook at those sneaky reporters. You know, one of those gossip columnists followed us to the supermarket yesterday and tried to chat up Suzie when I left the trolley for a moment in the confectionery aisle. The idiot even offered her a lollipop.' She ruffled the curly brown head leaning against her knee. 'Luckily Suzie blitzed him with her favourite word.'

Suzie blinked up at Rosalind, her blue eyes huge in her doll-like face. *'No!'* she bellowed proudly. 'No! No! No! *No!'*

Julia chuckled. 'She made such a racket that the guy had a hard time convincing everyone he wasn't a child-molester. I bet *that* put a crimp in his column!'

'He's lucky I wasn't there; I would have put a crimp in his face,' growled Hugh, whose gentleness was known to be in direct proportion to his size.

Rosalind smiled weakly, stricken by the thought that her uncompromising stance might have put the trusting innocence of her nephews and nieces in jeopardy. Typically, she had been so swept up in her own problems that she had taken her family's support for granted, without thinking how much it might cost them in terms of their own privacy.

Her certainty that she was doing the right thing by standing her ground dwindled further. Perhaps she *should* just abandon her principles and run for the hills... or rather the South China Sea.

It seemed such a callous thing to do while Peggy Staines still hovered between life and death in the intensive care unit at Wellington Hospital. But it wasn't as if Rosalind could provide any positive help for her recovery. Quite the reverse—knowing that she was around might cause Peggy to have another heart attack.

A brief word of sympathy with a distracted Donald Staines in the hospital waiting room was all that Rosalind had permitted herself. He had asked what had happened but not why, and Rosalind had caught a plane back to Auckland before he or any of the other members of the Staines family had rallied sufficiently from their shock to ask for the details. Until Peggy had recovered enough to carry on a lucid conversation—*if* she recovered—Rosalind was bound by her conscience to remain silent.

Thank goodness the police hadn't become involved, although Rosalind had the sinking feeling that if the publicity continued to escalate either they or someone involved in national security might feel obliged to come sniffing around with some serious questions, and then she might have no choice but to betray her conscience.

'Well, what do you say, darling?' her mother asked eagerly, visibly frustrated by Rosalind's lack of enthusiasm. 'I can't believe you're even hesitating...'

A disturbingly familiar tension began to crawl around the back of her skull as Rosalind looked into the expectant faces around her. A paralysing sense of her own vulnerability swept over her, but she knew she mustn't allow it to dictate her actions. She couldn't let the fear win.

Surprisingly it was Jordan who came to her rescue. Her brother-in-law rose to his feet, dominating the room with his muscled bulk, almost dwarfing Hugh.

'I think we should back off and let Roz make up her own mind in her own time,' he said with the ease of a man confident of his authority. 'She'd probably like to go home and think things over without the rest of us breathing down her neck.'

Rosalind cast him a grateful look and he continued smoothly, strolling over to take her by the elbow, 'Why don't I run you back to your apartment now, Roz, so you can do just that? Here, take these with you.' He scooped up a handful of brochures and thrust them into her free hand, and picked up her embroidered tote bag from a chair, looping it over her shoulder.

'You can leave your own car here as a decoy,' he said. 'The reporters won't bother to follow me if they see me leave alone. You can nip out over the back fence and through the neighbours' gardens and I'll drive around the block and pick you up in the next street.'

'Uh, but I'm going to need my car later,' said Rosalind, disconcerted by the unexpectedness of the offer and the firmness of the grip steering her towards the door. Although Rosalind and Jordan were cordial to each other, she had always been very careful to maintain a cool distance between them that had precluded friendship. Out of the corner of her eye she could see Olivia observing her husband's urgency with a worried crease of suspicion on her smooth brow.

'Richard or one of the others can drop it over to you later.' Jordan brushed aside the feeble protest. 'At least it'll give you a temporary respite from all the unwelcome attention you've been getting.'

The idea of a few hours' respite from the blood-hounds outside was undeniably appealing. 'Well . . . I suppose . . . OK, thanks.' She dug her heels in and skewed round to look over her shoulder. 'Uh, are you coming, Olivia?'

'Olivia wants to stay and chat with Connie, don't you, kitten?' Jordan cut in as his wife opened her mouth. 'We're going back to Taupo tonight and with her exhibition coming up she might not get the chance to visit again for a while...'

There was a hasty flurry of startled goodbyes as Rosalind found herself hustled out into the hall.

'For heaven's sake, what's the big rush?' she hissed as Jordan practically pushed her out the back door. 'Did you see Olivia's face? She looked awfully suspicious...'

'Maybe she thinks you're going to try and seduce me again,' said Jordan sardonically, blocking the doorway as she made a tentative effort to go back inside.

Rosalind, who never blushed, went hot at the reminder of one of the most mortifying encounters of her life. 'That was all a horrible mistake and you know it,' she gritted fiercely. 'I didn't know you two had even met when I pretended to be Livvy... and anyway, nothing happened—'

'Quite. There's zero physical attraction between us. I know it, you know it, and Olivia certainly knows it. After all, even when I thought you were her and *wanted* you to turn me on, you failed miserably.'

'OK, OK, I get the picture,' Rosalind grumbled, jerking her elbow out of his grip. 'But I might point out the failure was completely mutual.'

He grinned, his odd-coloured eyes warming with laughter. 'True. So now we've finally got that out in the open maybe we can relax around each other. Olivia is beginning to worry that we intend to keep up the pussyfooting for ever.'

Rosalind grinned back, relinquishing the last vestige of embarrassment which had constrained her natural, exuberant friendliness. 'Well, I guess if you can accept your total lack of sex appeal, so can I,' she teased with deliberate ambiguity.

'Big of you,' said Jordan, ignoring the overt provocation. 'Do you need a boost over that wall, or can you make it yourself?'

At five feet nine Rosalind wasn't used to men treating her as a wisp of delicate femininity and she reacted with her usual bravado to the implied challenge. Waiting in the quiet cul-de-sac on the other side of the neighbours' property a few minutes later, she brushed off her painfully grazed palms with a rueful acknowledgement that at her age maybe she should start thinking about putting dignity before daring.

Jordan's car turned out to be a macho four-wheel drive, scarcely less attention-grabbing than Rosalind's beloved fluorescent green VW, but, as he had predicted, the journalists outside the Marlows' gate had let him go unhindered when he had forced his way through the gauntlet of their questions.

'So...what's the real reason why you offered me a lift?' asked Rosalind quietly as they cruised towards the city. 'Don't tell me it was just to clear the air between us. You could have done that any time. It's something to do with Livvy, isn't it? Why she was looking so...*pulled* back there at the house...'

She watched Jordan's big hands tighten betrayingly on the wheel, highlighting the nicks and scars that were the legacy of his work as a sculptor.

'She's pregnant,' he said baldly.

The words hit her like a sharp blow. Rosalind's ears rang and she felt a chill across the base of her skull and tasted metal on her tongue.

'Pregnant?' she whispered. She felt a floating sense of utter separation. Olivia. Her sister. Her twin... the other half of herself... was going to have a *baby*... contribute to the growing brood of Marlow grandchildren?

Rosalind was shocked ... and more; emotions boiled through her that she didn't dare examine too closely.

'I thought she didn't want a family yet,' she said, when she could get her stiff mouth to work. 'She said she wanted to concentrate on her painting—'

'I know,' Jordan's voice was clipped and slightly grim. 'We agreed we were going to wait a few years ... but fate evidently had other plans for us. Olivia found out last week—she's still trying to come to terms with it herself; that's why she doesn't want to tell anyone just yet ... No one else in the family knows and she wants to keep it that way for another few weeks. Apart from her own ambivalent feelings, there are one or two early warning signs, like elevated blood pressure, that the doctor is nervous about ...'

Rosalind sensed rather than saw the sidelong look that Jordan gave her as he continued carefully, 'It's a little too soon to confirm it, but the doctor suspects from his physical examination that it could be twins ...'

*Twins.* Of course, given their family history, it was only to be expected, but Rosalind's sense of shock deepened. Livvy, the mother of not one child but *two*. The buzzing in her ears increased and she put her hand over her clenching stomach in sudden awareness. 'Livvy's been having dreadful morning sickness, hasn't she?'

'Yes; how did you know?'

Rosalind's mouth twisted. 'I've been a bit nauseous myself every morning for the past couple of weeks. I thought it was just nervous tension, or something I picked up doing that wretched film. The food was quite dreadful ...'

Pregnancy was the one thing that she *had* firmly been able to rule out from her self-diagnosis. Oh, God! Her skin prickled with fresh horror. What if she had to suffer these shadow symptoms all through Olivia's pregnancy? What an unspeakable irony that would be ...

'Well, Olivia's been as sick as a dog and the doctor's advised as little stress as possible in the next few weeks,' said Jordan bluntly. 'That's why I was hoping that you'd graciously accept Connie's offer. It would mean one less source of emotional turmoil for Olivia. If she thinks you're frolicking happily in some nice, safe tropical haven she might stop beating herself up that she's abandoning you in your time of need...'

'So much for your wonderful idea of whisking me away to make up my own mind in my own time,' said Rosalind, her sarcasm hiding a leap of relief that here was a cast-iron, honourable excuse for running away from her problems. If Livvy had a miscarriage, Rosalind would never forgive herself if there was even the slightest possibility that she was a contributing factor.

Jordan gave a rueful shrug. 'I didn't want to push it too strongly in front of Olivia. She wouldn't thank me for trying to protect her, especially if it compromises her loyalty to you. If you don't go to Tioman, Olivia intends to ask you to come and hole up with us at Taupo, even if it means dragging along your press contingent, not to mention your other little problem...'

Rosalind stiffened, her fingers clutching the seat as he suddenly swung sharply into a parking spot beneath the warehouse that housed her inner-city loft. 'What other problem?'

Jordan switched off the engine. 'You have so many you don't know which one I'm referring to?' he murmured, shaving much too close to the truth for her liking. 'I'm talking about the fan who's been making such a nuisance of himself.'

'Oh.' Aware of his shrewd eyes on her face, Rosalind tried not to reveal any of her turmoil as she probed warily, 'Olivia *told* you about that?'

She couldn't help a trace of outrage creeping into her voice, although, come to think of it, she had only asked

that her twin not tell their parents, or their over-protective
brothers.

'We *are* married, Roz,' said Jordan drily, effortlessly
picking up the nuances. 'That's what marriage is all
about—sharing a life, listening to each other's secrets
and worries. Olivia said you tried to treat it as a joke
but the mere fact that you brought the subject up made
her think you were a lot more concerned than you let
on, and the tenor of some of the guy's letters disturbed
her. She thought they could be interpreted as stalking
letters, said that he wrote as if he believed he had a personal relationship with you, one that gave him some sort
of a claim on you...'

'I told her I get lots of fans writing to me off and
on—'

'But this Peter is very persistent, Olivia said. You told
her it had been going on for several years, and that lately
he'd escalated from an occasional letter to one or two a
week, never with a full name or a return address. He
boasts of going to extraordinary lengths to see your per-
formances and even claims to have met you several times
at public appearances, though he apparently never
identified himself.

'Olivia said she didn't like the obsessive nature of his
interest, especially as he knows where you live. She said
you had extra locks fitted at your apartment because
you were uneasy when he started sending gifts as well
as letters. She also thought that one of the reasons you
took that film job in such a hurry was because you hoped
he might lose interest if you weren't performing live any
more...'

'Well, it was better than her idea of involving the
police,' Rosalind muttered, shuddering at the thought.
'They probably would have laughed in my face... there
was nothing in the letters that was overtly threatening.
Anyway, I've thrown most of them away,' she said
truthfully, hoping that would put paid to the subject.

'As I told Olivia, the best way to handle these things is to ignore them.'

'Mmm.' Jordan's face was sceptical. Rosalind had the sinking feeling that she had just acquired another over-protective relative.

'Nothing arrived while I was away,' she pointed out. 'Maybe he's finally given up.'

'And another sudden sojourn out of the country might be the perfect way to discourage him even further,' Jordan said smoothly. 'It's either that or the police, Roz—or I could get someone from the Pendragon Corporation's security section to provide you with personal protection while a private investigator tracks this guy down and turns him inside out.'

Rosalind blanched at the implications. 'Me, with a bodyguard? God, can you imagine what the Press would make of *that*?' She threw up her hands, hastily conceding defeat. 'You're something of a pirate, aren't you, Jordan? I suppose if I *don't* allow myself to be blackmailed into going I'll find myself shanghaied...'

'There's little I wouldn't do to ensure Olivia's well-being,' he agreed blandly, but with irrefutable honesty.

'Oh, all right!' At least he was allowing her to save face by pretending that she was doing this for her sister's sake, rather than her own. 'If I'm going to be shanghaied, I suppose I may as well make the most of it.' She grinned, her eternal optimism fizzing back to the surface. 'I might even find my own form of protection. Who knows? I might run into my *beau idéal* in paradise, a man "gentle, strong and valiant" who'll romance me under the tropical stars and pledge his heart to me for ever! Or, failing that, I'll settle for a gorgeously tanned beach boy who can make me laugh!'

# CHAPTER TWO

ROSALIND stood impatiently tapping her scuffed cowboy boot as she watched the man dithering at the check-in counter.

He was tall and thin, his thick, straight, mid-brown hair flopping over his forehead as he bent over to attach the tags to his two suitcases with fumbling fingers. He had a distracted, disorganised air that had Rosalind immediately pegging him as some sort of head-in-the-clouds academic, one of those people who were sheltered by their narrowly focused intellects from the real world— or perhaps he was a computer nerd, she thought as she noted the laptop he was carefully guarding between his feet. The jacket of his dark pin-striped suit fell open as he leaned forward and she saw the pens and folded spectacles tucked into the breast pocket of his white shirt. Ah, *definitely* a nerd!

Whoever he was, he was holding her up. Didn't he realise that first-class passengers didn't expect to have to *queue*? They were supposed to breeze in and out while staring down their noses at the lesser mortals lining up at the parallel desks.

She glanced around the terminal. She was anxious to be out of the public arena and into the relative privacy of the first-class lounge as soon as possible. She had got this far without being spotted, by dressing in androgynous jeans, baggy shirt and denim jacket and shaggy blonde wing *à la* Rod Stewart under a dark fedora.

She had swopped places with Olivia the previous night and knew her regular pursuers were being well and truly led off on the wrong trail, but news organisations often

27

employed stringers or informants at airports. In her boyish guise she hoped that no one would give her a second look, but the longer she stood around, the greater the risk of being accidentally rumbled before she boarded her seventeen-hour flight to Singapore.

The check-in clerk pointed at the weighing machine beside her desk but instead of obeying her polite instruction the man leaned forward to mumble something, patting absently at his pockets.

Rosalind's impatience burst its bounds. Stepping around a polite Japanese couple, she tapped the laggard briskly on the shoulder, lowering her naturally throaty voice an extra notch.

'Hey, mate, she's asking you to put your luggage onto the weighing machine.'

'What?' The man turned his head and his body followed, straightening with an uncoordinated jerk that caused him to almost fall over his laptop. Colour streaked across his high cheekbones as Rosalind snickered.

He was younger than his fussy mannerisms had led her to expect—about her own age, Rosalind guessed. His dark olive skin was unlined, and as he raked back his fine, straight hair with well-kept fingers he revealed an exaggerated widow's peak bisecting a smooth, deep brow. His face was narrow, his steeply slanting dark eyebrows peaking to sharp commas just beyond the outer corners of his eyes, giving his expression a strikingly devilish cast. However, the look in his dark brown eyes was anything but satanic. They were wildly dilated, watching with blank consternation as Rosalind snatched up one of his bags and plonked it onto the platform.

'She can't process you until you weigh your luggage,' Roz told him, her own eyes shooting impatient green sparks at him from under the brim of her hat as he made no attempt to follow her example. He was certainly slow on the uptake. If it hadn't been for that computer she would have thought he was two bricks short of a load.

Or maybe he was simply foreign, and didn't understand what was being asked of him.

He cleared his throat. 'Uh...I didn't think weight mattered for first-class passengers...' he murmured vaguely, his mild New Zealand accent immediately shattering her theory.

Rosalind's impatience drained away to be replaced by amused condescension. He was obviously a complete greenhorn.

'The airline still has to know what total weight the plane is carrying,' she pointed out. 'If you're packing elephants with your underwear they might have to shed a few economy passengers to accommodate your eccentricity.'

'Yes, yes, of course,' he muttered, not a glimmer of a smile touching his narrow mouth. She might have known he'd have no sense of humour. He continued to stare at her with the glazed abstraction of a man whose brain was temporarily otherwise engaged. To Rosalind, used to provoking sharp male awareness of her femininity, his lack of reaction was further proof of the effectiveness of her simple disguise. There were quite a few Shakespearian heroines who disguised themselves as boys, and Rosalind had played most of them with great gusto. She knew that gender confusion was largely a matter of body language.

She hooked her thumbs through the belt-loops of her jeans and widened her stance. 'Well?'

He blinked warily at her challenge. His lashes were surprisingly thick, veiling a subtle shift in his expression. 'Well what?' he asked guardedly, his fingers clenching convulsively around the blue travel folder he carried in his left hand.

His white-knuckled tension indicated that he was braced for some sort of scene. Did he think she was angling for a tip? Rosalind rolled her eyes and picked up his other suitcase. It was hefty enough to make her grunt, but her lithe body had the strength demanded by her profession and after staggering slightly she heaved it onto the platform next to the lighter bag.

'It was supposed to be a joke about the elephants,' she commented, panting slightly as she stepped back, tilting her chin to look up at him. 'What have you got in there, anyway?'

'Uh...books,' he said, still in that same thready voice adrift with uncertainty.

It figured. Her gaze swept the empty floor around his immaculately shod feet and a mischievous impulse prompted her to stoop for the case between his polished shoes.

At last she got an unequivocal reaction. 'No! Not my computer!' he exploded, grabbing it up and cradling it protectively against his chest like a baby. 'I'm carrying it on with me.'

So he *could* move faster than snail's pace when he wanted to! Rosalind grinned and tipped him a mocking salute on the brim of her hat.

'So it's just the two cases going through, then, is it, Mr James?' asked the airline employee with marked patience.

He didn't turn his head, seemingly hypnotised by Rosalind's cocky grin. 'Uh, well, I think...'

'He means yes,' Roz supplied firmly. She began to suspect that his air of muddled confusion presaged a man on the verge of panic. Perhaps the poor lamb was afraid of flying and was trying to put off the evil moment.

'Mr James? May I see your passport now, sir?'

'Passport?'

Rosalind decided it would be quicker for everyone if she took charge of the bewildered Mr James.

'You *have* remembered to bring it with you, haven't you?' she demanded, stepping up beside him at the desk. 'Is it in here?'

She plucked the blue folder out of the hand clamping the laptop to his chest and flicked it open to see an impressive wad of US traveller's cheques tucked behind the clear plastic pocket. He made a choked sound of protest and she gave him a chiding look to reassure him that she wasn't a thief. In the other side of the pocket was a slim dark blue cover stamped with the New Zealand coat of arms. She extracted it and, adroitly avoiding his belated attempt to snatch it back, presented it across the desk.

'Do you have any preference for seating?' she asked him, pushing the travel folder back into his hand as the woman leafed through his passport.

'I beg your pardon?' he said, his dark eyes flicking over her face in that irritatingly unfocused way, as if he still couldn't quite believe that she was helping him.

'You know—front seat, back seat, nearest the emergency door...that kind of thing?' she clarified.

'Emergency door?' he echoed, with a swift frown.

The frown had the decidedly odd effect of slanting his wicked eyebrows even more satanically without raising a ruffle on the angelically pure forehead. She wondered idly whether his personality contained as many contradictions as his face. He was actually rather good-looking in a limp-around-the-edges kind of way. At least a woman wouldn't need to fear being dominated by the force of his personality!

'Look, don't you worry about it, chum. Just leave everything to me.' She gave up trying to involve him in the decision-making process and negotiated his boarding pass without further consultation, thrusting his departure card and returned passport at him as the formalities were completed and nudging him away from the desk so that the Japanese couple could take his place.

'Well, go on, then,' she said to him, when he seemed inclined to hover inconveniently. 'You can toddle off to the departure lounge now.'

He didn't appear to recognise a brush-off when he heard one. 'Um, I thought I might wait for you...we could have a drink together—or something...' He trailed off vaguely, flapping his free hand in the air.

*Or something?* Rosalind studied him with sudden suspicion. Had he guessed that she was a woman, or did he think he was issuing an invitation to a pretty youth? Maybe that little-boy-lost helplessness was a sexual rather than psychological signal. Either way it was up to her to disabuse him.

'I wasn't trying to pick you up,' she said flatly. 'I helped you out because I felt sorry for you, not because I fancied you.'

He sucked in a sharp breath, a rush of blood darkening his skin. 'I wasn't—I didn't mean—'

His outraged stammer almost made her relent. Her initial impression had been right: harmless, prissy, easily embarrassed. But she still needed to get rid of him before she presented her own documentation. Under the country's privacy laws, airline personnel were forbidden to give out information about passengers, but if the woman mentioned her name out loud she didn't want anyone close enough to overhear.

'Good.' She cut him off, pointedly turning her slender back on him. 'Because I'm not interested.'

'I only wanted to thank you for coming to my assistance,' he said rigidly, and she grinned to herself at the hint of grit in his milk-shake voice. Maybe he wasn't such a hopeless wimp after all.

She didn't answer, and after a moment was relieved to hear him moving away. The trouble with helping lame dogs was that they had a lamentable tendency to want to cling to their rescuers.

After she had checked in she headed for the duty-free shop where she spied Jordan browsing amongst the perfumes. He was flying out to Melbourne on a short business trip related to an arts foundation created by

Pendragon Corporation and had conveniently saved Rosalind the taxi fare to the airport.

Their discussion of a couple of days ago having eased her awkwardness in his company, Rosalind gave in to impulse and crept up behind him and whispered menacingly in his ear. 'Poison!'

'Do you think so?' he murmured, withering her with his lack of surprise at her sudden ambush. 'I rather think that Livvy would suit something lighter, fresher...maybe Yves St. Laurent's Paris?'

As usual he was right. Rosalind waited while he bought the perfume and they chatted briefly before Jordan's attention was suddenly riveted elsewhere, his eyes slitting as he gazed intently over her head.

'What's the matter?' asked Rosalind, her overstretched nerves jumping. 'Who is it? A reporter?'

Jordan put a heavily reassuring hand on her shoulder as he shook his head. 'No, no—just someone I know from the old days at the Pendragon Corporation. I'd better go and have a word with him before he comes over and expects to be introduced.' He kissed her absently on the cheek, eyes still focusing beyond her. 'Have a good trip, won't you? And for God's sake try not to attract your usual quota of trouble!'

Rosalind bristled at that, and spun around as he left, intending to send him on his way with a few blistering words of self-defence, but at that moment she caught sight of the James man amongst the swirl of people in the public departure area. He was easily picked out—he looked isolated and alone in the midst of groups hugging and kissing their farewells. She hurriedly turned her back and skulked off to bury herself in a magazine in the relative privacy of the first-class lounge.

Rosalind didn't fully relax until she was on board the plane with the engines powering up. The first-class section was only half-full, which meant that those travelling alone had the added privacy of an empty seat beside them. Rosalind's assigned seat was an aisle one and she had decided to wait until they were airborne before she shifted to the window.

'Excuse me, Miss Marlow, would you like me to store your hat in the overhead compartment?'

'Thanks.' With a straight face Rosalind doffed her wig along with the hat, enjoying the flight attendant's classic double take. They both broke into chuckles and the hostess's mask of impersonal politeness was banished by the relaxed warmth of their shared moment of humour.

Rosalind's natural optimism raised its battered head. She suddenly felt freer than she had in a long, long time. No stresses, no awkward questions, no responsibilities. Maybe this holiday was just what she needed to get her life back on its former smooth-running track.

She sighed with satisfaction as she ruffled her flattened hair into its normal spiky style and accepted the suggestion that she might like a glass of champagne as soon as the flight took off. She stripped off her jacket and rolled up the sleeves of her green shirt, revealing a slender gold bangle on her left wrist.

Glancing at the seats diagonally behind her, she saw the ineffectual Mr James wrenching his seat belt unnecessarily tight, his mouth flat and grim, his precious computer sitting on the empty aisle-seat beside him. He was wearing dark-rimmed spectacles that gave his face a top-heavy look. Maybe it had been myopia rather than mental confusion that had led him to look at her so blankly in the terminal.

He was looking at Rosalind rather than concentrating on his task, and she judged from his frozen expression that he had seen her little performance with the wig and heard her womanly giggle. Evidently he wasn't a theatregoer, because there was no sign of slack-jawed recognition or avid curiosity in his regard, only cold disapproval, and Rosalind's sense of liberation increased. She gave him a provocative, feminine smile and a flutter of her dark lashes and he scowled, a muscle flickering in his cheek, his skin taking on a betraying colour. She had never known a man whose complexion was such a tell-tale barometer of his emotions.

As the stewardess swished past on the way to strap herself in for take-off, Rosalind attracted her attention and murmured, 'He's probably too embarrassed to mention it but I think Mr James back there might be a first-time flyer with a touch of phobia.'

The stewardess looked discreetly over her shoulder and made a swift professional assessment. 'Hmm, he does look a bit white around the mouth, and that case of his should be stowed away...' Her voice took on an unprofessional lilt of mischief. 'Cute, though. Maybe I'd better sit by him and hold his hand for take-off...'

She suited her action to her words and Rosalind couldn't resist watching the man's disconcerted expression as the attractive young woman stowed his computer and bent over to adjust his lap-belt before slipping into the vacant seat beside him and enveloping his hand in a manicured grasp. She said something to him that made his head jerk up. He pushed his spectacles up his nose and shot an accusing look in Rosalind's direction that was a surprisingly fierce mixture of frustration and annoyance. Rosalind beamed him a plastic smile. Ungrateful nerd!

Dismissing him from her mind, Rosalind settled in to enjoy the flight. She had never flown first class before and intended to take full advantage of the shameless pampering. Some of the pampering involved the liberal distribution of newspapers and magazines and Rosalind almost choked on her champagne when she spied a photograph of herself cavorting on the front cover of a local popular women's magazine. She quickly took it for herself and confiscated several other magazines that she suspected might carry news of her current notoriety in their pictorial gossip columns.

Unfortunately her clumsy attempt at censorship was thwarted by the fact that the other stewardesses were offering an identical selection to other passengers. Taking a furtive peep around the cabin, Rosalind was relieved to note that most of the others were selecting more edifying reading ... business reviews and glossy fashion magazines ... except for the wretched James man, who received a copy of every single publication and then proceeded to open the very one Rosalind was hoping would be beneath his intellect to notice.

Rosalind muttered to herself as she slid over into the window-seat, out of his sight-line. Maybe he wouldn't make the connection—the cover photo was years out of date, taken when she'd still had long hair. What kind of man picked a women's magazine as his first choice, anyway? And did he *have* to hold it up in such a way that his fingertips appeared to be tucked into an intimate portion of her bikini-clad anatomy?

Thinking she might as well know the worst, Rosalind thumbed open her own copy and read the three-page story, torn between anger and amusement to discover that it comprised euphemistically couched rumours of her bisexuality, supposedly dating from the time that she had 'eagerly' accepted a lesbian role on stage. There was an illustrated list of all the men with whom she had been 'romantically linked', which seemed to consist of every male celebrity with whom she had ever been photographed, and to that list was now added a gaggle of 'gal-pals'.

Turning the page in fascinated awe at the artistry of the inventions, Rosalind learned that she was now on the 'hot list' of a radical gay organisation that focused on outing famous people and that she was on the verge of accepting an offer to appear as the nude centrefold in a famous men's magazine.

Unfortunately this time it wasn't only her own somewhat tarnished reputation at stake. Thanks to the country's strict libel laws, there wasn't one mention of Peggy Staines, but she would obviously be in the mind of any reasonably informed person who read the story.

If only Rosalind hadn't agreed to meet Peggy at that hotel! If only Peggy hadn't insisted on such extremes of secrecy, even down to registering the room in the damning name of Smith. If only Rosalind hadn't been so stunned by the older woman's private revelations that she had ignored the first signs of her distress and then wasted precious time searching Peggy's bag for her medication instead of calling the emergency number straight away.

Rosalind struggled against a renewed flood of guilt. None of it had really been her fault, she reminded herself. She had made a few mistakes in judgement, that was all. She might have been a principal player in the drama, but she hadn't been its author. It was Peggy who had written the original script, and in spite of her sympathy for the woman Rosalind couldn't help resenting the fact that *she* had somehow ended up as the scapegoat in the tangled affair.

She stuffed the offending magazine into the pocket on the seat in front, determined not to brood. Rosalind's philosophy of life was simple: be positive. There was no point in agonising over actions and events that couldn't be changed. Self-pity got you nowhere but in the dumps. You had to keep moving forward, substitute 'if onlys' with 'what ifs' and regard each negative experience as character-building for the future rather than as a destructive barrier to present happiness.

With that firmly in mind Rosalind shucked her boots off in favour of the free airline bootees and prepared to eat and drink and make merry across several thousand kilometres of airspace. If she was going to zonk out on a beach for three weeks she had no need to worry about jet lag!

Her body, however, had other ideas. The stresses of the last couple of weeks and the strain of the past few months caught up with her, and after a superb dinner accompanied by a few more glasses of champagne Rosalind found her eyelids drooping and her mind pleasantly unravelling.

She snuggled under a down-soft blanket and fell asleep watching a movie she had particularly wanted to see, and when she awoke was disorientated to find herself muffled in total darkness. She fought her way free of the blanket covering her face and found that the cabin lights had been dimmed and almost everyone else was asleep. The attendants were murmuring in hushed voices in the curtained galley.

Feeling a pressing need, Rosalind stumbled blearily into the aisle, staggering slightly as the plane hit mild turbulence. Not quite everyone was asleep, she found as she groped her way sleepily towards the toilet. The James man's bent head was burnished by a pool of light, revealing glints of red-gold amongst the nondescript brown strands which had slipped forward to mask his tilted profile. As she passed his seat she saw that his laptop was open on his unfolded table and that in his hand he was holding...

'Are you *crazy*?' Rosalind lurched forward and snatched the object from him. 'Have you been using this?' she whispered, shaking the cellphone accusingly in his startled face.

'I—'

'Didn't you read the safety information? Don't you *know* it's prohibited to use portable phones on board planes?' she hissed.

'Well, I—'

Rosalind glanced around to see if anyone had noticed and crammed herself down into the seat next to him.

'They can play havoc with the plane's electronic systems,' she told him, speaking quietly so as not to disturb the sleeping passengers around them. But even in a whisper her classically trained voice retained its full range of articulation and expression. 'If anyone had reported you, you could be arrested as soon as we land...that's if you don't cause us all to crash first!'

His eyebrows rose above the straight line of his spectacle frames at her fiercely delivered lecture. 'Are you going to report me?' he asked curiously.

She was offended by the suggestion. 'Of course not!' She was still slightly muzzy with sleep but he looked disgustingly bright and alert as he studied her expressive face. For a fleeting moment she thought she glimpsed a smouldering rage in the dark eyes, but when he blinked it was gone and she decided that it must have been a trick of the light.

'There's no "of course" about it,' he said evenly. 'You might have found it amusing to get me into trouble with the authorities—'

Her snort of indignation was genuine. 'You must have a very odd idea of my sense of humour. I don't happen to think it's funny to mock the innocent.'

'Is that what you think I am? An innocent?' His mild voice sounded hollow, incredulous even. No doubt in his own mind he was a witty, sophisticated man of the world... The imagination had wonderful ways of compensating for one's personal inadequacies!

'Well, an innocent abroad, anyway,' she said, humouring him. 'It does rather stick out: you didn't know about not using portable phones...or about the check-in procedures, and you were practically falling to pieces with nerves at the airport—'

'Perhaps I was merely stunned speechless by your beauty.'

His sarcastic retort left her unruffled. She knew she wasn't beautiful in the classical, restrained sense but she had flamboyant good looks that most men found attractive and an innate sense of style. 'You thought I was a boy,' she reminded him smugly.

'Did I?' he murmured quizzically, leaning back in his seat so that his face moved out of the spotlight. Thrown into shadowed relief, his features were stripped of gentleness, imbued now with a brooding strength that seemed vaguely sinister. A man of dark secrets and intriguing mystery...

'You know you did,' she said, admiring the effectiveness of the illusion: comic relief as villain. She had always believed that lighting was more effective than make-up in creating a character and here was the proof.

He said nothing and she frowned, suddenly remembering the magazine he had been leafing through at the beginning of the flight. Her pride bristled. Damn it, if he was toying with her over the matter of her identity...!

'But you obviously know who I am now, right?' she challenged.

His eyes dipped to her breasts, which were barely visible under the loose drape of her shirt, and to the slender curve of her hips, spanned by a wide leather belt which emphasised the narrowness of her waist. His gaze travelled down further, to the cellphone resting on her upper thigh, next to where the snug V of her jeans was pulled flat across her pubic bone.

'Yes...you're obviously a woman.'

The stifled statement was somehow more flattering than a gush of admiring words. To her surprise Rosalind felt her body tingle as if he had physically touched her where his eyes had wandered. Usually perfectly comfortable under the most leering male appraisal, she hurriedly crossed her legs in an unconscious gesture of self-protection.

A woman. If all she was to him was an anonymous female then he hadn't paid much attention to that magazine, she thought with relief. He'd probably just skimmed over the glossy pages of celebrity clones before tossing it aside.

She looked at him through her lashes and received another small shock. Instead of politely averting his gaze, he had allowed it to linger on the deepened V created in her lap by her crossed legs, almost as if he could see the transparent emerald lace bikini briefs she wore beneath the sturdy denim. The muscles along her inner thighs tightened with a feathery ripple and she instinctively sought to shatter her unexpected self-consciousness with flippancy.

'Those aren't X-ray glasses by any chance, are they?' she joked, and his eyes jerked back to hers. 'Or are you going to confess they're just plain glass and you're simply a mild-mannered reporter?'

'I beg your pardon?' His eyes looked like polished jet—or perhaps it was just a coating on his spectacle lenses that made them look so hard.

'You know—like Superman?' He looked at her steadily and she let out a huff of disbelief. 'For goodness' sake, you don't have much of a grasp on popular culture, do you? What do you do for a crust?'

'Crust?'

She rolled her eyes. 'A living? What sort of job do you do?' She leaned sideways to peer at his laptop, to see if it would give her a clue. She glimpsed a busy clutter of characters before, with the swift tap of a single finger, he closed the file he had been working on, leaving the cursor blinking on a blank screen.

'Top secret, huh?' she teased, tilting her head back, the light flaring to fierce brilliance in her short cap of red hair.

'Something like that.'

She shrugged good-naturedly at the rebuff. 'Oh, well, we all have our secrets.'

'Some more dangerous than others.'

The idea that his vague and distracted manner was a cover for a life riddled with dangerous secrets tickled her funny bone. 'Ah, don't tell me...' Her voice dropped to a bare whisper as she rasped behind the back of her hand, 'You're really a spy travelling to the mysterious East on a secret mission of national importance!'

She ruined the blood-curdling effect with a husky chuckle. 'A spy's who's afraid to fly!'

His colour rose. 'I'm *not* afraid of flying.'

'Of course you aren't,' she said, deadpan. 'The stewardess only held your hand for take-off because she thought you looked cute.'

'*You* told her to do that,' he accused through his teeth.

'Oh, for goodness' sake, that was only because I knew you were probably too shy to ask for help. She came up with the "cute" all by herself—'

'Too *shy*?' He looked as if she had hit him over the head. Did he think it didn't show?

'Well, you must admit you don't have a very...um...*assertive* personality, do you?' she said tactfully, patting his arm. It felt surprisingly solid under the dark fabric. Unlike the other men in the cabin he had not removed his suit jacket but merely loosened his tie and a couple of shirt buttons. Through the sagging gap in the crisp white shirt she could see the smooth, surprisingly tanned skin of his chest. No hairy he-man he, she thought with an inner giggle.

'Not that there's anything wrong with being shy,' she continued as he glowered at her. 'A lot of women find that endearing in a man...you know, a nice change from the swaggering macho come-ons. You shouldn't feel embarrassed about asking for help when you need it, though. People respect you more for admitting your weaknesses than for trying to hide them behind a mask of false bravado. It takes courage to let people know that you're vulnerable—'

'I don't *need* anyone's help.' He interrupted her homily with an exasperated snap. 'I don't know where you get your ideas but I can assure you Miss—' He stopped abruptly and sucked in a sharp breath. 'Miss...?'

'Marlow,' Rosalind offered quickly, anxious that his sudden burst of self-assurance should not be undermined by a minor point of etiquette.

'Miss *Marlow*,' he accepted grittily, without a flicker of reaction to the name. 'I can assure you that if I am ever in need of assistance I am perfectly capable of arranging for it by myself!'

'Excuse me!' It was one of the stewardesses, speaking to Rosalind in a sternly admonitory tone. 'That's not a portable telephone you've got, is it?'

Rosalind sensed the man beside her stiffen, as if he expected her to leap at the chance to rat on him. He was probably honest to a fault. Left to himself he would doubtless pour out a full, frank and totally unnecessary confession.

'Yes, but don't worry, I'm not using it,' she said swiftly, with a winsome smile. 'Mr James here has been showing me his state-of-the-art travelling office. I was just holding this while he demonstrated some dazzling technical wizardry on his computer.' She cast him a look of patent awe before switching her attention back to the object of her persuasion. 'Naturally the phone is switched off,' she said, hoping it was. 'We're both well aware of the airline regulations.'

'Hmm, well, just to be on the safe side, perhaps we should remove the batteries to prevent it becoming accidentally operational.' The stewardess smiled, whisking it from her and deftly opening the panel. 'Oh, someone's done it already...'

A masculine arm brushed against Rosalind's breasts as the telephone was firmly retrieved by its owner. 'Yes, *I* did—prior to take-off. As Miss Marlow pointed out, I'm fully aware of the current regulations.'

'You might have told me,' Rosalind protested in chagrin as the stewardess glided away. She scrambled to her feet, acutely conscious that her breasts were humming from his unexpected touch.

'You didn't give me a chance to get a word in edgewise. You were having too much fun jumping to conclusions and patronising my ignorance,' he said sardonically.

Rosalind was tempted to flounce off, except that what he said was perfectly true. Her green eyes sparkled as her mouth curved self-mockingly. 'I was, wasn't I?'

A twitch of his extraordinary brows showed that her ready confession was unexpected, and evidently unwelcome. 'You also lie extremely well,' he accused unsmilingly.

His chilly disapproval earned him a taunting little bow. '"If I chance to talk a little wild, forgive me; I had it from my father,"' she said sweetly. The obscure Shakespearian quotation was certainly apt—she had learned much of what she knew about acting at Michael Marlow's knee...including how to make blank verse sound like modern, everyday speech!

He gave her a darkling look, as if he suspected that the lyrical apology was not her own and was frustrated by his inability to challenge her sincerity by quoting its source. She had already guessed that Mr James liked to be safely armoured head to toe in facts before he proceeded into verbal engagements.

Unable to resist rubbing his nose in it, she placed a hand over her heart and flaunted a more recognisable quotation. 'Ah, "parting is such sweet sorrow", isn't it, Mr James?' She batted her eyelashes shamelessly at him. 'But now I know that you're such a boringly well-organised individual I suppose I'll have to find someone else to patronise. Enjoy the rest of your trip. Ciao, baby.'

She turned and sauntered on her way, making sure she gave her hips an extra swivel just in case he was still watching.

He was, and it was fortunate for Rosalind's peace of mind that she couldn't see the expression on his face. It was a mask of cold-blooded calculation, the mouth a cruel, hard line of satisfaction, the eyes hot and hungry, seething with an unstable combination of unwilling admiration and reluctant contempt.

The bitter face of a man on a particularly unpleasant mission.

And who was determined to succeed.

# CHAPTER THREE

ROSALIND clamped her shoulder bag to her side as she jogged across the shimmering tarmac towards the small, colourful, twin-propellered aircraft. A steamy, swirling Singapore wind whipped her hair into a red halo as she cast an angelic smile of apology at the uniformed airline officer standing beside the lowered steps at the rear of the fuselage. She had been deep in conversation with a young German tourist when she had realised she was going to be late for her connecting flight. She had made it with barely thirty seconds to spare!

The door was pulled smartly shut behind her, shutting out the baking afternoon sun, and Rosalind's smile swept around the narrow, nineteen-seat cabin before zeroing in on the gap halfway up the left-hand side of the aisle. She eased herself between the rows of single seats, scattering apologies as her bag banged protruding elbows, and crammed herself gratefully into her seat. She could see the pilot looking back through the open door of the cockpit and she gave him a cheeky thumbs up.

'You nearly missed the flight.'

Rosalind looked across the aisle into a pair of familiar, dark, disapproving, bespectacled eyes.

Oh, no! The insipid Mr James was a reminder of the country and complications she was trying to escape.

'Don't tell me *you're* going to Tioman too,' she blurted out as the plane began to vibrate with engine noise.

'No, I'll be parachuting out halfway there,' he said drily.

Considering that they were on a non-stop, terminating flight, his sarcasm was justified, but just as Rosalind

46

was appreciating his glimmer of wit he spoiled it by adding ponderously, 'That was rather reckless of you, cutting it so fine. You could have wasted your ticket.'

'Nonsense; I had it timed perfectly to the last second,' she lied airily. 'When you've flown as often as I have you'll realise that there's an art to minimising boring waiting times.'

'Right,' he murmured, eyeing her flushed complexion, slicked with perspiration from her dash to the plane, and the green shirt which clung in interesting patches to her dampened skin.

Rosalind rummaged in her bag and produced a moistened towelette which she used to blot her face, uttering a sensuous sigh of pleasure as the cooling alcohol evaporated on her hot skin. He was still in his suit, she noticed, although he had removed his jacket and tie as a concession to the heat; his ubiquitous laptop was jammed under his feet. Was he going to work all the way across the South China Sea, the way he had across the Pacific?

Curiosity—her besetting sin—got the better of her. If she was stuck with him as a seat companion for the next hour or so she might as well make the best of it.

'What a coincidence we're both going to the same place,' she remarked as the plane taxied down the runway. 'Are you going there on business or pleasure?' she asked, although she thought she knew the answer. Nobody went on holiday wearing a suit!

'You might say a bit of both,' he replied. One corner of his narrow mouth indented briefly, as if he was restraining a smile of grim anticipation. He obviously wasn't expecting to enjoy himself much on either score.

'And what exactly is your business? You never did say...' Rosalind trailed off invitingly.

He hesitated. 'I'm an accountant.'

'Oh... really?' Rosalind managed to keep a straight face but she quickly lowered her eyes, knowing they must be brimming with suppressed laughter. 'I never would have guessed.'

She didn't fool him one bit. His jaw stiffened. 'You find my profession amusing?'

'Of course not; accounting is a very serious, very honourable, highly regarded profession,' she said earnestly.

'Don't overdo it,' he warned her wryly.

She let him see her dancing eyes as she burbled, in a little-girl voice of breathless admiration, 'And so exciting, too. You must get a big thrill whenever you get your accounts to balance.'

His expression was stoical. 'My accounts *always* balance.'

He managed to make his conscientiousness sound like a threat. It was too much for Rosalind's sense of humour.

'So many thrills, so little time!' she giggled. 'No wonder you look so strung up. You have all the hallmarks of a workaholic. I won't ask you what your pleasure is; it probably has something to do with that laptop. I bet you have no idea how to really kick back and relax. Where are you staying on Tioman?'

When he named the resort her first reaction was amused resignation. So much for her flippant 'Ciao, baby'. It seemed that they were fated to run into each other.

'Me too.'

As the words left her mouth a nasty suspicion began to buzz crazily in her head. Ridiculous as it might appear, maybe coincidence had little to do with it...

'Are you following me?' she rapped out.

He looked so alarmed at the prospect that her brief attack of paranoia subsided as abruptly as it had arisen. He was an accountant, for goodness' sake! He wore a *suit*, and an expensively tailored one at that. All the tabloid journalists Rosalind knew—and she knew some of them on a first-name basis by now—dressed for comfort and climbing walls rather than for impressing their quarry with their sartorial elegance.

They didn't travel first class, either, and in the unlikely event of managing to persuade his tight-fisted employer to spring for a ticket no self-respecting hack would have piously waved away the free booze every time it was offered, as she had noticed Mr James do.

'I think you'll find I was the first person to check in for the connection and I was certainly on board this plane first,' he pointed out with the stiffness of outraged innocence. 'How could I possibly be following you?'

Quite. Remembering what her mother had told her about the underdeveloped nature of Tioman, Rosalind conceded that of course anyone who travelled first class would inevitably stay at the island's most luxurious hotel. She tried to smooth his ruffled dignity with a mischievous, melting look.

'Mmm. How indeed? Maybe *I'm* the one following you...'

He blinked rapidly, blurring the expression in his dark eyes. Rosalind noticed a small tick in his left temple and realised that her provocative reply had only made him even more uncomfortable. He jerked his face away from her scrutiny, glancing out of his window just as the nose of the plane lifted, his fingers gripping the armrest as the ground fell sharply away beneath them and they shuddered across the heatwaves rising from the city.

Rosalind looked at the white knuckles. Maybe it wasn't her teasing banter that had made him poker up so suddenly.

'Flown much in small planes, have you?' she asked with studied casualness, determined not to make the same mistake she had on the flight from Auckland.

He wrenched his gaze reluctantly away from the window and gave her a wary, sidelong look as if he still didn't know quite what to make of her. Did he expect her to pounce on him and start ripping his clothes off?

Or perhaps he was afraid to admit his vulnerability because he thought she would mock his fears. She smiled kindly, encouragingly, determined to make up for embarrassing him with her absurd suspicions.

His eyes narrowed on her eager, enquiring expression. 'Not a great deal, no,' he admitted slowly, surprising her, for she had half expected a snub.

Rosalind beamed at him and adopted a bracing tone. 'Well, don't worry; the ride'll smooth out when we get up a little higher. And we'll leave the up-draughts behind once we get over the sea. The flight's not much more than an hour long. We'll be there in no time. If your ears start to hurt, suck one of these.' She whipped out a few boiled lollies from the fistful she had pocketed on their previous flight and held them out to him. 'Sorry if they've melted a bit but they're still in their wrapping so you won't get sticky.'

He accepted the peace offering, picking out the paper-sealed toothpick with the airline logo which had been hidden amongst the sweets and gravely handing it back.

'Surely you want to keep your souvenir, Miss Marlow?'

She grinned sheepishly as she dropped the toothpick into the breast pocket of her shirt. 'It's the bargain-hunter in me, I'm afraid. I just can't pass up a free offer. I can never leave a hotel room without making a clean sweep of the teabags and coffee sachets and the soap and little bottles of shampoo. Things like that are built into the room rate, you know, and they can be very handy when you're living on a budget.'

His eyebrows rose steeply. She was beginning to get rather fond of them. They were his most expressive feature.

'A very poorly balanced budget, Miss Marlow, that affords first-class travel but leaves you insufficient funds to buy the small essentials of life.'

She grinned at his professional criticism. 'I didn't say I *couldn't* afford them; it's only that I'd rather spend the money on other things. Actually, this whole trip is a gift. Normally I'm strictly a second-class traveller. And my name is Rosalind by the way. Most people call me Roz.'

No dawn of recognition crossed his expression, no glimmer of licentious speculation intruded into the clear dark gaze.

'Luke James.'

There was a pause, almost as if he expected *her* to recognise *him*. Maybe he was famous in accounting circles.

She prodded him further. 'I'm an actress.'

'I'm afraid I'm not much of a movie-goer,' he began politely.

'I work mostly in the theatre.'

'Or a theatre-goer either.'

'I did have a leading part in a BBC costume drama a few years ago—'

'I don't own a television set,' he said without regret.

'Oh. Well, I've done a number of radio plays—'

'I rarely have the radio on...'

Rosalind was stunned. How could someone of his evident education have no interest in or appreciation of the dramatic arts? Didn't he know that the theatre provided both a window and a mirror to humanity? How could he consider himself a well-rounded personality if he ignored such an influential part of his cultural heritage?

She scowled. Perversely, considering the lengths that she had gone to in the last twenty-four hours to avoid being recognised, she felt slighted by his complete lack of awareness of her talent. She wasn't overly big-headed, but she knew that she had earned every one of her glowing reviews. She worked hard and believed passionately in the importance of her craft. And yet here was a man who didn't even *care* about what she did, let alone how well she did it!

It was on the tip of her tongue to ask whether he read the newspapers, but she wasn't prepared to go *that* far towards betraying herself.

'Well, then, what *do* you do for entertainment?' she asked, hiding her chagrin.

'I don't feel the need for it. My life is very full.'

'It must be,' she said tartly. Full of work, she guessed disparagingly. Parades of dull, unimaginative figures marching across his computer screen. Her generous lower lip pushed out moodily, her green eyes darkening as she contemplated the philistine across the aisle. No wonder he didn't interact very well with people, poor lamb. He lacked the practice in sharing his emotions which was normally imparted by exposure to common cultural experiences. If variety was the spice of life, his must be singularly bland.

'I'm sure you're a very good actress.'

Her trained ear detected the dubious note in the comment that was obviously meant to mollify her.

'How would you know?' she pointed out sarcastically.

'Well...' He lowered his voice, his gaze fixed on her stormy face. 'You *are* very attractive...'

Rosalind bristled like a ginger kitten whose fur had been stroked the wrong way. 'What's that got to do with how well I can act?' she crackled.

'Uh, I... suppose it must make it easier for you to get parts,' he explained.

Did he realise what he was implying? Could those brown eyes really be as innocent and guileless as they seemed? Rosalind bristled even more fiercely. 'You mean sleep my way into them—is that what you're saying?'

Her bluntness had the desired effect. He blinked rapidly. 'Oh, no... I would never suggest such a thing. Uh, I'm sure you're a very respectable, very distinguished actress.'

Rosalind was as quick to forgive as she was to anger. She was aware of the irony, even if he wasn't. Her ire dissolved in a gamine grin.

'Now who's overdoing it? I think you must be confusing me with my mother. Dignity is not exactly my strong point and respectable I ain't! I will, however, concede that my *work* is respected.'

In case her wordplay was too subtle for him she added firmly, 'If I sleep with someone, it's because I want to, not because I have to. As far as I'm concerned, sex is not a marketable commodity.'

Surprisingly he neither blushed nor looked flustered by the raw revelation. Onc eyebrow flicked up. 'Your mother is also an actress.'

Given his cultural ignorance, Rosalind treated it as a question. Connie would have been mortified that he had had to ask. She had been playing leading roles for nearly four decades. The Marlow name was a byword in the New Zealand theatre. Rosalind felt honour-bound to defend the family pride in its accomplishments.

'Yes. Constance Marlow.'

She half expected him to look blank but instead he dipped his head in acknowledgement.

'You're one of *those* Marlows. Didn't your father receive a knighthood for services to the theatre in the last honours list?'

Where art failed, snobbery succeeded!

'Yes, he did.' The new title had been the source of some mirth as well as pride within the family, since Michael's bark had frequently reduced quavering young newcomers to calling their director 'sir' and Connie had been going under the affectionate theatre nickname of Her Ladyship for years.

'I suppose *your* mother is an accountant?' she teased, basking in the safety of her clan. As 'one of those Marlows' she was shielded from the infamy of her individuality.

Again that slow, assessing look. 'My mother died when I was a child.'

'Oh.' Rosalind's amusement was instantly tempered, her jewel-bright eyes softening sympathetically. 'I'm sorry. What a shock that must have been.'

Her vivid imagination sketched a picture of what he had been like as a child. He would have been a thin, clever, gentle little boy, too shy to attract many friends and, after the loss of his mother, probably even more insecure. She couldn't imagine Luke as the kind of self-confident daredevil that her brothers had been ... or herself, come to that.

Impulsively she spanned the aisle with her slender arm and placed her hand over the one lying on his seat-rest. The back of his hand felt cool and hard against her palm, as if the tanned skin were sheathing cold steel rather than warm muscle and sinew. Rosalind had somehow expected that an accountant would have hands that were soft and pampered. Maybe it was all that exercise on his computer keyboard that made his fingers feel as if they were capable of cracking walnuts!

Even more disconcerting, the hum of the aircraft was transmitted to her via her touch—a prickling vibration which shot from the point of contact right up the length of her arm, raising the fine hairs on her skin as if it were charged with electricity.

Luke looked down at the small, pale, delicate hand cuddled protectively over his.

Absorbed in her imaginative reconstruction of his orphaned boyhood, Rosalind missed the significance of the slight, premeditated pause before he added with stark pathos, 'It was an accident. My father died too.'

Her hand contracted, along with her tender heart, her fingers curling comfortingly between his. The engine hum in her arm increased to a steady tingle that spread up her shoulder and down over her collar-bone. 'You were an orphan? Oh, Luke...how awful for you. Do you have any brothers or sisters?'

He turned his head. She was leaning towards him, her vibrant restlessness momentarily subdued by the desire to comfort, her creamy skin pale with the intensity of her feelings, her beautiful eyes wide with anxiety and muted with sorrow.

All for a virtual stranger.

Where in the hell were her self-protective instincts? wondered Luke James with a savage dissatisfaction. Damn it, she was making this *too* easy...

Or was she? Luke had good reason to know that she wasn't as vulnerable and unsophisticated as her tender expression of compassion invited him to believe. Her apparent openness was an illusion. To an actress of Rosalind Marlow's calibre the lies would come tripping off the tongue. He might admire the act, but he didn't have to believe in it.

'No. No one.'

The tight-lipped answer touched a painful chord inside Rosalind. She couldn't imagine life without her large, loving family. The chord continued to resonate, reaching deep into the secrets of her soul.

She could see the awareness of his loss still there in the back of Luke's eyes, the ghostly reflection of an old bewilderment. And, behind that, an even deeper, colder, darker emotion that she couldn't identify.

'Relatives? Surely you had *someone*...?'

There was a palpable tension in the set of his shoulders. 'I was fortunate to be adopted,' he said tonelessly, sliding his hand abruptly out from under hers and placing it out of reach in his lap.

'I'm glad,' said Rosalind quietly, undismayed by his physical withdrawal. Some people were natural touchers and others weren't. The Marlows were an expressive lot, both physically and verbally.

'Everyone should have a family, don't you think? Even if it's an artificially constructed one,' she continued, her smile tinged with a fleeting wistfulness. 'It's our family that teaches us to expect love and trust and loyalty from those around us, so that when we go out into the world we're not afraid to pass on our trust to others, to admit that we're all interdependent...'

'Ask not for whom the bell tolls...' he murmured.

'Exactly! Although, actually, it's "never send to know for whom the bell tolls; It tolls for thee",' said Rosalind, a stickler for getting her lines right. She was delighted to find out that he had at least a passing acquaintance with poetry. Perhaps he was still redeemable. 'Have you read much John Donne?'

'Enough to misquote him occasionally. The remnants of a classical education.'

'Oh? Where did you go to school?'

He named a private boys' school, famous for its academic excellence and strict code of behaviour—also for the level of its fees. She wondered whether his parents' estate or his adoptive family had paid for his education.

'Were you a boarder?' she contented herself with asking.

'Yes, I was.'

He uttered the words with pride, but Rosalind thought that packing young children off to live in institutions was a barbaric practice and said so. She shuddered delicately. 'All the Marlows went to a state school, thank God, where we were relatively free to express our individuality. I could never have stood boarding-school. All those petty rules and restrictions. I would have rebelled simply on principle.'

'Your parents didn't set restrictions on your behaviour when you were a child? They didn't expect you to adhere to minimum standards of decency and self-control?'

There was a bite to his questions that made her a trifle defensive. The Marlow brand of home discipline might have been liberal but it had never been lax. 'Yes, of course they did, but their rules were tempered with heaps of love and humour and a very broad tolerance, and we weren't threatened with expulsion from the family if we did something wrong!'

'I was never threatened with expulsion either.'

'Probably because you never dared do anything wrong,' dismissed Rosalind knowingly. 'How did you manage in the dorm? Aren't boarding-schools filled with budding little sadists and thugs who lord it over everyone younger and weaker than themselves?' Her voice acquired a pitying husk. 'You must have suffered more than your share of bullying—'

'Must I?' he interrupted crisply. 'Why?'

'Well, you're not exactly built like a rugby player, are you?' she said frankly, giving him the once-over. As her eyes settled back on his face she noticed his heightened colour and the tell-tale rigidity of the muscles in his jaw and— Uh-oh, she must have bruised his masculine sensitivities!

'Actually you're a bit like my brother Richard,' she said hastily. 'He got picked on for being a gawky kid— all elbows and knees and a chest like a chicken—but he wasn't feeble by any means and the older he got, the more he appreciated his natural leanness. Women positively *drooled* over him when he got into the movies—'

'How very reassuring, but your concern for me is quite misplaced,' Luke said, with a cutting precision that rejected her backhanded compliment. 'I was never a particular target for bullying, nor, I'm glad to say, indiscriminate drooling, which sounds equally unpleasant.'

His words had more impact than he could know. Rosalind let her bright head drop back against her seat with a sigh.

'Oh, it is, it is,' she said moodily, thinking of all those salacious tales about her which had floated to the surface over the past week. She had once thought such rumours funny, hadn't minded people entertaining themselves with silly exaggerations about her sex life. But the joke had somewhat lost its savour when it had become coupled with the knowledge that somewhere out there beyond the spotlight was a faceless man who regarded her as his own personal possession, who was obsessively collecting every scrap of knowledge about her, watching, waiting, gradually shaping and fashioning her to fit his private fantasies, turning her from a person into a . . . a *thing* that he might one day come to claim, perhaps violently . . .

And because of that life would never be the same for Rosalind. She would never again feel quite as safe, never be quite as carefree and trusting as she once had been. Olivia had been frustrated by her twin's refusal to take Peter seriously, but Rosalind had always handled her fears and doubts by laughing at them, by holding them up to ridicule and contempt, because to do otherwise would be to admit that they had unreasonable power over her.

But this time her tried-and-true remedy had failed her. She had received a harsh lesson in helplessness that she had longed to repudiate. That was why she had gone streaking down to Wellington after that tantalising telephone call.

'We've never met,' the woman had faltered, after introducing herself only as Peggy, 'but I believe we have a mutual . . . friend—someone who's been writing a lot of letters to you lately—someone I'm worried about.'

Rosalind's heart had accelerated and she'd gripped the receiver hard. 'You're talking about Peter?'

A deep, unsteady breath along the line had signalled her caller's mingled nervousness and relief. 'Yes. You obviously know who I mean. But I... I don't want to get him into trouble...'

'Nor do I,' said Rosalind honestly. 'I haven't made any sort of official complaint yet, if that's what you're asking. I was hoping the situation would resolve itself...'

'Maybe it will. It's just—I saw some of Peter's letters to you, at his flat... I found photos, and things of yours—he has a whole *room* wallpapered with pictures of you; it's almost like a shrine the way it's set out. I think he's more likely to harm himself than anyone else but I— You see... Oh, it's so *complicated*...you can't possibly imagine! I—I thought that you and I might be able to help each other, to help *Peter*, without there being a fuss or any ghastly publicity—'

She broke off with what Rosalind thought sounded like a sob but then continued, her voice choppy with distress. 'It's all so very *awkward* talking like this over the phone. This is terribly *personal*, you see, Miss Marlow. Not even my family knows—they *mustn't* know—'

Rosalind could hear the incipient panic building. Her informant sounded almost at the end of her tether. She might lose her courage any moment and hang up, leaving Rosalind none the wiser as to her, or Peter's, true identity.

'I agree; nobody else has to know. Would it make you more comfortable if we could meet, Peggy, and talk about it face to face?' she interrupted gently, clamping down on the impulse to hammer urgent questions down the line. 'Just the two of us, alone? Trust me, I don't want any unnecessary publicity about this either.'

'Oh, yes, could we do that?' There was a gushing sigh of immense gratitude. 'But it needs to be right away and I live in Wellington...' Her voice swept high again in tense frustration. 'My husband is in the Government, you see, and our comings and goings are sometimes monitored. I don't have any excuse to come to Auckland at short notice and the family is bound to be curious and suspicious if I suddenly take it into my head to insist...'

The woman's ragged dignity and desperation triggered Rosalind's compassion as well as her avid curiosity, especially after hearing that she was the wife of Donald Staines, a conservative pillar of the political establishment and self-appointed watchdog of New Zealand morality.

Reading between the lines, Rosalind guessed that Mr Staines was an authoritarian husband who lived by a set of rigid, old-fashioned standards and expected his wife to be equally upright and unblemished in character. He had no truck with modern, namby-pamby psychology that forgave people their sins because they had been victims themselves, and, whatever Peggy's involvement with Peter, it was obvious she feared she would receive contempt and condemnation rather than help and understanding on the home front.

Rosalind had just got back from location. She had hardly even unpacked, but she didn't hesitate. She threw a few things back into her bag and flew to Wellington that very evening, booking into the agreed meeting place as the ubiquitous 'Miss Smith'. She was eager to shrug off her growing sense of powerlessness by seizing the initiative and taking assertive action instead of passively waiting for events to run their own course.

The hasty trip turned out to be a massive error in judgement. Perhaps if she had been more sensible and less arrogant, and had sought professional advice before rushing off to slay her phantoms, then Peggy Staines would not have had her heart attack, or the accompanying stroke which had complicated her recovery.

Hell!

The burden of guilt now resettled crushingly on Rosalind's shoulders. It all came down to choices and Rosalind knew that in the last few weeks she had made too many of the wrong kind: wrong personal choices, wrong career choices. Just about everything she did these days was turning out *wrong*, she thought, heaving a luxurious, self-pitying sigh.

'Rosalind? Are you feeling ill?'

She blinked and discovered that she had been frowning blankly out of the window of the plane at the vast blue nothingness. The sky was utterly clear, not a wisp of cloud in sight, and as her eyes dropped Rosalind could see the flattened contours of the Malaysian countryside below.

A broad brown river snaked lazily across the blue-green landscape, looping back on itself to almost enclose fat teardrops of lush jungle. Where the jungle gave way to serried ranks of palm trees she could see narrower brown bands—dirt roads running in straight lines for kilometres through the vast palm-oil plantations. From above, the palms looked like clusters of multi-armed starfish, spreading their green limbs across the earth-bed beneath a crystal-clear sea of air.

'Rosalind? Is something wrong? Why are you looking like that?'

The harsh demand shattered her abstraction. She looked around. Luke James had removed his glasses and his naked eyes weren't the least myopic as they drilled into hers. They were razor-sharp with curiosity, and with a jolt of alarm Rosalind recognised a shrewd intelligence at work. She hoped he wasn't as perceptive as he was evidently observant.

'Sorry...what was it we were talking about?' she said, instinctively brandishing the shield of charming vagueness that had served her so well in the past. 'I'm afraid my thoughts wandered off on a tangent. I tend to do that sometimes—my imagination is pretty wild...'

He refused to be diverted. 'Not very pleasant thoughts, whatever they were. From your expression, I thought the wing must be on fire at least!'

That explained his uncomfortably dissecting look. She must have given him a scare! Her mouth relaxed into a teasing curve.

'Believe me, if anything was wrong with the plane you'd be getting a far more extroverted performance than a dreamy stare out of the window! I'm a stage actress, remember? I'm trained to dramatise events and exaggerate emotions. You can't judge me by ordinary standards of behaviour...'

He frowned, replacing his spectacles. Rosalind could see disagreement seeping into his expression and another question forming on his stern lips. For goodness' sake, couldn't he take the hint and lighten up? She wasn't in the mood for serious conversation. She was having a holiday from deep and meaningful discussions!

Determined to thwart him, she steamrollered on in a relentlessly light and frivolous vein until she saw his eyes begin to glaze over and his jaw stiffen against a yawn. Only when she was certain that she had successfully bored him to distraction did she lapse into silence. She turned back to the window to hide a small smile of satisfaction as he quickly opened his laptop on his knee and buried his nose safely in his own business again.

She took a crumpled flight magazine out of the seat pocket in front of her and pretended to read, but as the plane angled out across the South China Sea she found herself seduced by the hypnotic flash and leap of the sun, dancing dimples of silver brilliance across the restless blue mantle. An occasional small fishing vessel and, as they neared Tioman, a sprinkling of raw, windswept rocks and tiny green-tipped islands jutting out of the sea provided the only visual interruptions.

The plane banked for its approach and Rosalind caught her first glimpse of their destination. The narrow tongue of land widened as the plane continued to turn, revealing the full vista—low, rock-strewn cliffs rising to steep, jungle-clad slopes which marched upwards and onwards into the hazy, mountainous interior.

She pressed her nose against the window so that she could watch as the tumbled boulders and stony cliffs gave way to long, wide streaks of smooth, pale sand. The exotic greenery grew thickly to the very edge of the beaches, and was broken only here and there by clearings for human habitation.

They descended further, flying across a bay where a long white jetty jutted out across the water. In the space of a few minutes the sea had changed dramatically, from a solid, opaque blue of fathomless depths to an exquisite, translucent cobalt as it skimmed over the sandy shallows to melt with scarcely a ripple onto the silky beaches.

Exactly like the brochures! Rosalind thought with a rush of pleasure, sending out a mental apology to her mother for doubting that her enthusiasm would bear comparison with reality.

The airport, when it hove into view, was tiny—a couple of alarmingly short concrete runways nestling at the base of the forested hills. A quicksilver thrill of exhilaration threaded through her veins. She couldn't help a quick glance over at Luke James to check how he was coping with the idea of landing in a patch of cleared jungle the size of a postage stamp.

He wasn't. Instead, he was watching her, his back turned to the solid wall of greenery now whipping past the window. She was surprised by his cool composure until she realised that his fixed fascination was more likely to be a state of controlled panic. By focusing his concentration on Rosalind he was blocking out his awareness of what was happening outside the plane.

Her own eyes were vividly bright, betraying the love of excitement that was intrinsic to her impulsive nature.

By the time they had bumped down onto the uneven runway and shuddered to a smooth halt beside the small, open-sided wooden building which served as a terminal Rosalind's earlier annoyance with Luke was forgotten in her eagerness to explore her new environment.

'It wasn't so bad after all, was it?' She grinned at him as they carried their bags the few metres from the shady terminal to the narrow, dusty road just outside the chain-link gates. 'I thought that landing was going to be a hair-raising roller-coaster ride, but it was actually quite smooth and easy.'

'Yes, I could see you were disappointed,' murmured Luke acidly as he set his suitcase down under the shade of a leafy palm and watched most of their fellow passengers board a small blue and white resort bus parked outside the wire gates.

'Well, maybe a little bit,' she confessed, looking around for their own transport. 'I happen to love roller coasters.'

'That figures.'

A typical accountant's reply, thought Rosalind in amusement. Everything reduced to numbers. He'd probably never even been on one himself. Roller coasters definitely came under the heading of entertainment!

She strolled over to where a snazzy-looking red motor scooter was leaning against one of the fence posts and ran her fingers wistfully over the white seat. 'You don't suppose...?'

'No, I do not!' He gave her hopeful suggestion short shrift.

'Pity,' she said, imagining how good the breeze would feel as they zipped along in the open. The air around them was very sultry and still, and she could feel the sweat beginning to trickle down her spine. She fanned herself with her hat. She couldn't wait to get into her bikini and fall into that azure sea.

They didn't have long to wait. Just as the resort bus pulled away a large green and silver open-topped Jeep with a palm-tree logo embossed on the door tooled up in a cloud of dust and a slim young Malaysian man dressed in cool whites vaulted out with profuse apologies for his lateness. He had had to stop to assist a tourist who had had an accident with his bicycle.

'I am Razak,' he said, his dark, almond-shaped eyes widening at the sight of Rosalind's hair glowing like molten lava in the full glare of the sun. 'From the Tioman Palms...and you are Mr and Mrs...?' He paused to look at the clipboard he had tucked under his arm.

'He's definitely a Mr but I'm still a Miss,' Rosalind laughed. 'We're not married.' The idea was deliciously absurd.

'Oh!' Razak's curious gaze darted from Rosalind's irrepressible grin to Luke's smooth, unrevealing visage. He looked down at his list and frowned. 'But—'

'We merely travelled on the same flight.' Luke cut him off abruptly. 'We aren't together. We're total strangers to each other.'

His attempt to distance himself from her provoked Rosalind into pure mischief.

'Yes, Luke and I have never seen each other before in our lives,' she purred, with an innocent flutter of her lashes that was more telling than any number of torrid looks.

A faint flush rose on Luke's neck as Razak regarded him with a brief flare of masculine envy before hurriedly consulting his list and ticking off their names.

'If you'd like to get into the Jeep, I'll just go and find the other two people I have come to meet,' he said as he loaded their bags and directed them to the open back seat. 'Please enjoy the ride. There is very beautiful scenery all the way to the hotel...'

*Everything* was beautiful, thought Rosalind an hour later as she stepped out onto her bedroom balcony and inhaled a heady brew of tropical scents. The hotel accommodation consisted of a sprawling arrangement of wooden chalets, each containing two-storeyed suites. The rooms themselves cleverly combined stark simplicity with exquisite luxury, so that the guests could pretend that they were roughing it without suffering any of the attendant inconveniences.

By leaning further over the sturdy balcony rail Rosalind could see past the thicket of towering coconut palms and weeping casuarina trees to the broad white smile of the beach with its scattering of wooden sunloungers and huge, thatched umbrellas.

She turned her head at the sound of a slight scrape, and sighed as she saw a man leaning over the rail of the next-door balcony, which was screened from hers by a wooden lattice panel thickly covered with a glossy dark green creeper.

Instead of some exciting, sexy, fun-loving foreign millionaire, her neighbour was an accountant with an overdeveloped intellect and an underdeveloped social life.

Luke James had a lot to answer for!

# CHAPTER FOUR

HIS luck certainly wasn't improving, thought Rosalind in exasperation as she watched the slinkily clad woman sidle away from the man at the bar with an insincere smile pinned to her glossy lips.

She just couldn't take it any more. She picked up her tall glass and sauntered over to plonk herself down on the next bar stool.

'You really have to do something about that technique of yours,' she announced.

Luke James stiffened, almost spilling his drink as he turned towards her, his dark eyes flicking over her shimmering green tube-top and flimsy wraparound skirt before darting past her to the crowded table of laid-back revellers which she had just abandoned.

The fiery sunset had provided a magnificent backdrop for diners at the hotel's open-air terrace restaurant but the thick, velvety darkness had long since fallen and most people had drifted away to the disco or to watch the nightly 'entertainment extravaganza' provided by staff and local cultural groups. Others, pursuing quieter interests, were strolling the moonlit beach, or entertaining privately in their chalets.

'I beg your pardon?'

Rosalind plucked a cherry from the bristling array of fruit decorating her Mai Tai, tossing it into her mouth and enjoying the lush burst of alcoholic flavour on her tongue as she studied his wary expression with faint amusement. She couldn't blame him for being suspicious; after all, she had been rather obviously ignoring him ever since they'd arrived.

But she had magnanimously decided to stop trying to avoid him. In a resort as small and exclusive as the Palms it was virtually impossible anyway. Instead of fading obligingly into the background in the past couple of days, eclipsed by the far more colourful company at the hotel, Luke James had managed to snag at her attention constantly. He was almost always alone, undoubtedly hampered by the shyness which those who didn't know him might easily interpret as off-putting aloofness.

Rosalind felt sorry for him, aware of his frequent, surreptitious glances in her direction. While she had been merrily acquiring new friends and acquaintances with her usual speed he had remained uncomfortably out of place amidst the relaxed holidaymakers. At least tonight he had left his laptop in his room—this afternoon he had been using it under one of the umbrellas down on the beach, a solitary figure absorbed in his own little world, seemingly oblivious to the fun going on around him. The man obviously needed taking in hand!

'Your technique for picking up women,' she explained, licking her cherry-slick fingers. 'Although I must admit you seem to have the picking-up part down pat. It's what happens afterwards that seems to be your problem.'

'Afterwards?' His winged eyebrows whipped into a steeply defensive slant.

Rosalind's eyes creased with amusement as she realised that he had placed a sexual connotation on her innocent words.

'After you've delivered your opening lines,' she said demurely. 'You're supposed to follow them up with some witty banter that fans the sparks of attraction into a mutual conflagration. You're acting more like a wet blanket than a bellows. What made her suddenly change her mind?'

'Who?'

'*Her.*' She jerked her head in the direction of the woman who had now zeroed in on another solitary male at the other end of the open-air bar. 'The hot-looking lady who was chatting you up just now.'

'She wasn't chatting me up,' he denied irritably. 'We were merely having a polite conversation.'

Wow! Talk about being uptight! Rosalind rolled her eyes at his obtuseness. '*She* bought *you* a *drink*, for goodness' sake; how much more of an invitation do you need?' She tilted her bright head towards him, lowering her voice confidingly so that he had, perforce, to lean towards her. 'She was coming on to you, Luke—I recognised the body language even if you didn't. She was zinging you with those coy up-and-under looks, snuggling up to your side, making sure you got an eyeful of that impressive cleavage... and there you were, as stiff as a post—'

'I *beg* your pardon?'

Rosalind collapsed into giggles at his outraged growl.

'I meant your *facial* expression,' she told him when she'd finally managed to stuff the laughter back down her throat. 'The way you were holding yourself.' She went off into another spate of giggles, almost falling off the stool, as she realised she had uttered another unintentional *double entendre*.

He looked as though he would like to throttle her, had he possessed the courage. 'Really?' he muttered sceptically through clenched white teeth.

'Yes, really. I...er...kept my body-language observations strictly above the waist,' she said, straight-faced, and then she couldn't resist teasing him by looking down at his shoes and stroking her gaze slowly up the long masculine legs, encased in pale cotton trousers, which were wrapped around his bar stool.

All his casual clothing had an expensive kind of crumpled elegance that suited his lanky frame. He looked a far cry from the dithering nerd-in-a-suit she had met at the airport, but that was still the image of him that she carried foremost in her mind. However, she had noticed on the beach that his modest swimming boxers exposed some surprisingly well-defined leg muscles and her breath caught in her throat as her eyes reached his splayed thighs and the taut fabric across his hips revealed another unexpectedly well-defined aspect of his masculinity.

Her eyes skipped a survey of his short-sleeved white shirt and shot to his face, which, she discovered with a jolt, looked as heated as she felt. His slight flush gave her back the confidence to laugh huskily, as if she hadn't almost been hoist by her own petard.

'So...one minute you and she are having a nice, polite conversation and the next she's backing off as if you have the plague,' she said, propping her elbow on the bar and picking out more fruit from her glass. 'You were the one doing most of the talking. What on earth did you *say* to her?'

His eyes narrowed as he watched her devour a slice of pineapple with voluptuous pleasure. 'If you must know, I was merely telling her about one of my more intricate cases.'

The pineapple nearly flew out of her appalled mouth. *'Accountancy?'* she squeaked. 'You have a beautiful woman flirting madly with you and you talk *books and ledgers*?'

'It was a very interesting case,' he said mildly.

'Maybe to another accountant! She wasn't, was she...an accountant, I mean?'

'She said she was an exotic dancer.'

There was a small, incredulous silence. 'Safe to assume she isn't one of life's intellectual giants, then,' Rosalind said drily. An exotic dancer on the make and Luke had managed to let her slip through his fingers. If he had *tried* he couldn't have done a better job of lousing up!

'For goodness' sake, couldn't you find something more exciting to talk about... like the weather?'

'But she asked me about my work,' he protested.

'Yes, but she didn't really want to know all the gruesome details,' Rosalind told him. 'It was just an opening gambit, like asking what star sign you are or whether you have a light for her cigarette...'

'I don't believe in astrology and smoking damages your health.'

Rosalind kept a firm grip on her sense of humour. This was going to prove more of a challenge than she had thought. 'Do you have to take everything so *literally*? Boy, do you ever need help! Luckily I'm on hand to give you a few lessons.'

'Lessons?' His hair was ruffled by the warm off-shore breeze, a few glossy strands stirring and lifting to fall forward in twin curves on either side of the central widow's peak. He looked endearingly untidy for a few seconds before an absent hand slicked his hair back into its former neatness. Rosalind resisted the urge to reach up and restore the tousled look, which softened the sweeping angles of his narrow face and made him look more relaxed and casual...even rather sexy in a rumpled kind of way!

'In the fine art of flirtation. And don't say you don't need any because tonight was a rerun of what happened to you last night at the poolside buffet and today on the beach: initial feminine advance followed by hasty retreat. So far you seem to have a perfect strike-out rate where women are concerned.'

'I didn't realise anyone was keeping score,' he said tightly.

'Just call it a neighbourly interest.' She grinned, draining the rest of her drink. 'Don't take it too personally. People-watching is one of the accepted pleasures of being on holiday. The trick is not to let the watching take the place of healthy interaction—'

'Of which *you've* been having plenty, without apparent discrimination against age *or* sex!' he shot back. His mouth immediately compressed, as if he was angry at himself for the acid outburst. Following his brooding gaze to the uninhibited group of men and women with whom she had enjoyed her dinner, Rosalind guessed that his words had been prompted by a combination of wounded male pride and envy of her easy popularity. She forgave him instantly and defused the comment by dropping into character.

'Mmm, being irresistibly likeable is *such* a trial,' she drawled in an impeccable aristocratic whine. 'One is constantly in demand, but one must do one's duty, mustn't one, dear chap? *Noblesse oblige* and all that...'

Anyone else would have gratefully picked up the cue to gloss over a *faux pas*, but Luke's smile was a perfunctory twitch. 'I'm sorry if I offended you. I didn't mean to imply that I thought you were promiscuous.'

Didn't you? popped into Rosalind's head as she met his unblinking gaze and wondered at the challenging gleam in the obsidian depths. But then she noticed his hands swivelling his drink round and around on its paper coaster, and the tension inherent in the gesture reassured her that the defiant glimmer in his eye was merely a reflection of one of the flaming torches which provided the hotel's beach frontage with its romantic ambience.

She sighed and shook her head. 'You take life too seriously, Luke—no wonder you're having trouble handling a simple holiday flirtation! Unless... You *are* interested in women, aren't you?'

Now he did blink, shattering the illusion of steely-eyed concentration. His olive skin darkened a tinge. 'Of course I am!'

'These days it pays to check.' She grinned, patting his bare forearm. She was surprised to feel the same electric hum that she had felt when she'd touched him on the plane. Last time she'd put it down to engine vibration;

this time it must be the delayed punch of the Mai Tais she had been drinking.

'So, Luke,' she said, removing her hand and flexing her tingling fingers, 'do you want my help or not?'

His look, under the reckless brows, was unreadable. 'And if I said "not"?'

She tilted her chin and stared down her pert nose at him. 'Then naturally I'd steer clear of you for the rest of my stay. After all, I wouldn't want to interfere with your enjoyment of the wonderful, fun-filled, friend-crammed holiday you appear to be having.'

She wasn't surprised to see a brief flare of alarm in his eyes. 'Er... exactly what would this "help" of yours entail?' he enquired cautiously.

'You mean what would you be letting yourself in for?' The temptation to be outrageous was too much. She batted her eyelashes at him and said throatily, 'Why don't you buy me a drink, big boy, and find out?'

'*Big boy?*' He was startled into a dark chuckle. It was smooth yet rasping, a very masculine sound of appreciation that was all the more appealing for its undertone of reluctance.

At last she was getting somewhere! 'Too blatant?' she asked impishly.

'Erina was much more subtle,' he admitted, hiding the curve of his mouth against his glass. Rosalind watched the transparent liquid break against his lips and thought that if he was running true to form he was probably drinking mineral water.

'Oh, right! Miss Exotic Dancer was subtlety personi-fied... in a dress that was cut to her navel!' she said sarcastically. 'What did *she* call you?'

'Darling.'

Rosalind snorted, conveniently forgetting how often the word was abused by her profession. 'How hack-neyed. She obviously has no imagination. No wonder you gave her the brush-off.'

'It was vice versa, remember?'

'Only because you didn't give her a chance to glimpse the debonair man of the world beneath the accountant,' she said, already busily working out scenarios in her head.

He looked down into his glass, obviously struggling with some strong emotion. Gratitude, probably, thought Rosalind. 'It's very kind of you to take pity on me, but I don't like to encroach too much on your own holiday...'

'Oh, it won't take me more than a few days to whip you into shape,' said Rosalind confidently, wishing he would be less self-effacing.

'It sounds painful.'

'Stop being so negative. It'll be fun! You get a chance to explore your hidden potential and I get to play *Pygmalion*.'

'As long as you don't start giving me elocution lessons,' he said, so drily that for once she missed the joke.

'Oh, no, your speaking voice is one of your strong points...smooth and mellow, with just a hint of gravel in the undertone. And you have a sexy little hitch to some of your words. No, we definitely want to keep the voice.'

One eyebrow rose in an ironic slant, independent of the other. 'Thank you.'

Rosalind was impressed afresh by the whimsical charm of those wayward brows. 'Stick with me, kid, and this time next week women like Erina will be *begging* you to debit their balance sheets!' She gave him a lascivious wink and was amused to see him flush as he uttered another abrupt, almost unwilling laugh. It gave her a surge of odd, almost possessive satisfaction to watch his tightly compressed personality visibly unfold, although he obviously had a long way to go yet!

'I'm scarcely a kid,' he said stiltedly.

'Why, how old are you?'

'Twenty-eight.'

'Wow! *That* old, huh?' Dancing green eyes mocked his claim to maturity. 'How old do you think *I* am?'

His eyes flicked over her with unflattering speed. 'Thirty-five?'

'Ouch!' She laughed. With her supple, energetic body and elfin features she knew very well that she looked younger than her years. She licked her finger to place an imaginary stroke beside him in the air. 'Score one to me, Grandpa. I'm twenty-seven.'

'So I should be the one calling *you* kid,' he shot back with commendable speed.

'I may be younger in years but I suspect I'm decades older in worldly experience.' She chuckled, slyly swiping his glass in lieu of the Mai Tai he had failed to replenish. He made a half-hearted attempt at retrieval which she avoided by leaning back, giggling when the tube-top stretched alarmingly low over the smooth swell of her breasts, threatening to let them pop free. He froze and she directed a teasing look at him over the brim of the stolen glass before throwing back her head and dispatching the contents in a single swallow.

Mineral water it was not!

Rosalind choked on the ball of fire that exploded when the thick, oily fluid came in violent contact with the back of her throat, and grabbed gratefully at the cocktail napkin that appeared under her streaming eyes.

'My God, what in the hell was that?' she spluttered when she had recovered sufficiently to discover she still had a voice, albeit one that was cracked and croaky.

'Russian vodka, straight.'

Rosalind shuddered. 'You drink it raw? What are you, some kind of masochist?'

'It's an acquired taste, I agree.'

'Acquired taste! It's amazing you have any tastebuds left after drinking that stuff. It's like liquid fire. And it has a kick like a kangaroo!'

'I have a high tolerance for alcohol...something to do with my biochemistry, I believe.'

Trust Luke to have a boringly logical explanation for his dangerous taste in drinks. 'Lost opportunity there, Luke,' she chided wheezingly. 'You should have hinted at a shadowed past...that you *may* have acquired your liking for Russian vodka in Moscow, but the circumstances are not something you're at liberty to discuss.'

'You mean I should lie?'

'I said *may*, didn't I? It's not lying, exactly. It's weaving a romantic tale around the truth to make it a bit more interesting.' She sniffed. It was a mistake. The potent fumes lingering in her throat expanded into her nasal passages and made her eyes water furiously again. She abandoned the ridiculous argument over semantics and mopped at the brimming tears before remembering that she had applied a bold amount of mascara to her dark-brown-dyed eyelashes to make them look thicker and longer. 'Oh, no!' She raised her face to his. 'Has my mascara run?'

'Yes.' There was a trace of malice in his inspection. 'You look like a racoon.' She scowled at him and he tagged on hurriedly, 'A very pretty racoon, of course.'

She was torn between laughter and offended dignity. 'Oh, nice save, Mr Suave. Very debonair!' She slid off her stool. 'Since I haven't got my instant-repair kit with me I'd better take a face-saving stroll back to the chalet.'

Luke rose, sliding a discreet tip across the polished wood of the bar. 'I'll come with you. After all, it was my vodka that did the damage...and I wouldn't like anyone to take a swipe at you in the dark, mistaking you for a pretty, noxious pest.'

Rosalind groaned. 'You pick up the art of stinging banter awfully fast for a beginner. I hope I'm not unleashing a monster on the unsuspecting women of the world!'

'Perish the thought, Dr Frankenstein,' he murmured in her ear as they turned onto the crushed-shell pathway that branched off under the palms towards their small grouping of chalets.

When they reached her chalet she lingered on the doorstep, relaxed in the certainty that her escort wasn't suddenly going to turn into an over-amorous octopus. If there was any pouncing to be done she suspected she was the one who would have to do it!

Smiling at the thought, she ordered him to call for her the next morning, so they could plan out their day over breakfast at the elegant little coffee-bar on the balcony of the hotel's marine sports pavilion.

'But—'

'But what?' she said impatiently as she opened the door. 'You don't eat breakfast?' She turned to look at him, standing at the bottom of the wooden steps. 'Or did Erina make you a more attractive offer? Were you planning on having breakfast in bed, maybe?'

She couldn't see, because his face was shadowed by the night, but she would have bet that he was blushing as he growled, 'Of course not. I just wondered why it had to be so early, that's all.'

'You'll see.' She grinned and turned to trundle upstairs to the bedroom, uttering a shriek of horrified mirth as she saw her black-ringed eyes in the bathroom mirror. Rosalind Racoon indeed! Ah, well, tomorrow she would get her revenge . . .

She scrubbed her face till it was pink and shiny and fell into bed, drifting off to sleep to the hushed sounds of the sea and the tropical night breeze whispering in the palms outside her window.

# CHAPTER FIVE

ROSALIND woke to a furious thunderstorm.

No, not thunder. It was definitely a man-made racket, she decided as she opened her eyes to a room awash with light. Someone was hammering at the front door of the chalet.

Rosalind sat bolt upright and immediately fell back on the pillows, groaning, but it was too late—her stomach had already been set in unsteady motion. Waves of nausea washed over her and she closed her eyes, swallowing frantically, trying to think calming thoughts, but it was difficult to concentrate with the thumping going on downstairs, the sound vibrating through the wooden walls of the chalet. She held off for a few more miserable seconds but then had to make a heart-pounding dive for the bathroom.

She only just made it. She slumped to her knees by the toilet bowl, retching violently, feeling the sweat break out all over her tortured body. Even when she could bring up no more she still retched. She flushed the toilet and moaned as the churning of the water triggered a fresh bout. Death seemed a very attractive alternative.

The thumping had stopped and suddenly she became aware of a questioning voice echoing inside the chalet.

'Uh . . . Rosalind? I'm here! Are you ready to go?'

Luke! She lurched to her feet. She could hear the footfalls crossing the polished wood floor below. His next call was stronger as it came floating up the narrow stairway.

'Rosalind? Are you still up there?'

In a panic, Rosalind realised that if he came up the stairs he would find her in the nude. She preferred to sleep without the rumble of the air-conditioner and it was too hot to wear anything in bed but the flimsy sheets. She tried to call out but her voice emerged from her burning, bile-coated throat as a dry croak. She grabbed the green hotel robe hanging on a brass hook on the wall and wrapped it around her, her fingers fumbling with the tie as she staggered towards the door.

'Rosalind? I can hear you moving around; I know you're awake. Please, won't you answer me?'

'Yes, yes, I'm here.' She hurried down to meet him, moving as fast as she dared, a supportive hand sliding along the wall to give her stomach the illusion of stability. As she had feared, he had already started up the stairs and they met on the small landing.

Luke looked insufferably fit and healthy in white trousers and a rather vivid island-print shirt, the jewel-bright colours stamped on a red background—a garment which at any other time she would have coveted. As it was, its vibrancy made her stomach wince and she quickly shifted her gaze. His damp hair was neatly combed back, his recently shaven jaw was smooth and glossy and the crisp, clean tang of a citrus-based cologne preceded him.

In contrast Rosalind felt grubby and smelly and desperate for a shower, and when Luke froze in his tracks she knew that she looked exactly the way she felt. She glared at him, wishing she had long, abundant curls to hide behind, rather than the perky, short, nakedly revealing cut that she ordinarily loved.

'I'm sorry; I overslept,' she rasped sullenly. 'Did you have to pound at my door like that? I thought it was an earthquake.'

His speculative dark eyes roamed from her bare toes curling against the cool floor to the sleep-crease marring one creamy cheek. 'You told me to be here at this time.

I thought you meant that you'd be ready and waiting.'
He looked at his watch—a menacing lump of black
plastic studded with buttons. Why was it that the people
who needed them least always boasted the most macho
time-pieces? thought Rosalind sourly.

'So? Sue me,' she grunted.

'Are you always this grouchy in the morning?' For
some reason the notion seemed to give him pleasure.

'No. I'm usually much worse,' she snapped.

He nodded, as if he could quite believe it. 'You left
your door unlocked? Don't you think that's a bit unwise
for a woman alone?'

'I do now,' she said, unable to think of anything
wittier.

He looked at her as she leaned limply against the
painted wall, and moved tentatively closer. 'Are you sure
you're all right? Your face doesn't look so good.'

No wonder—her stomach was still trying to push itself
up into her throat! 'Gee, Luke, you really know how to
turn a girl's head.'

'No, I meant you don't look well,' he said. 'Have you
changed your mind about an early breakfast? Last night
you said something about bacon and eggs and waffles
dripping with syrup—'

'Oh, God!'

Rosalind clapped her hand to her mouth and whirled
about. She raced back up the stairs, almost killing herself
as she tripped over the trailing belt of the huge, one-
size-fits-all robe. This time she only made it as far as
the hand-basin, hanging onto it for grim life as she was
shaken by another bout of violent nausea.

Lost in her misery, she was barely aware of the long
arm swooping around her until it contracted to a tight
band just beneath her breasts, gently supporting her bent-
over body while her trembling legs were braced from
behind by the warm cup of masculine hips and thighs.
After she had finished her ignominious performance

Luke forced her to sip a glass of water so that she could rinse the vile taste from her mouth.

Rosalind, a notoriously bad patient at the best of times, was purely ungrateful.

'Go away,' she groaned thickly as she tried to wrestle herself free of his tender mercies. Either she was as weak as a baby or Luke was a great deal stronger than he looked. 'Why can't you leave me alone? I don't want you here. I don't—mmph, mmph...' Her fretful wail was smothered in the folds of a deliciously cool flannel as it was firmly stroked over her sweaty face and then her hands.

'I can do that myself.' She glared at him from under damply spiked lashes and ruffled brows dyed the same colour.

'Too late; it's done. Come on. Back to bed.'

He was very good at giving orders all of a sudden, she thought grumpily, but still felt too fragile to make an issue of it. She meekly lay down on the tumbled bed and closed her eyes. She felt the mattress alongside her hip depress with Luke's weight as he sat down on the edge of the bed.

'I think I'll ring down to Reception for the hotel doctor. If you have food poisoning it could be serious—'

'Don't bother; I know what it is and it's *not* food poisoning,' she roused herself to protest.

'Oh. I see.' Luke's slow enunciation dripped with distaste. 'Perhaps a hair of the dog would help, then?'

Rosalind's eyelids cranked open to check the disapproving slant of the demon eyebrows. 'It's not a hangover, either,' she retorted. 'I wasn't drunk last night. You should know; *you* walked me home...'

'You could have gone out again after I left. Or hit the room-service bar.'

Maybe someone he knew was an alcoholic. It was the only reason Rosalind could think of for his unflattering suspicions. 'Well, I didn't. I went straight to bed.'

'Then why are you ill?'

'I just got up too suddenly, that's all,' she muttered petulantly. He would probably laugh if she told him. Hell, *she* would laugh if this was happening to someone else. But right now she didn't feel in the mood to provide anyone with amusement.

He frowned, propping one hand beside her head and leaning forward for a closer inspection of her unhealthy pallor. His hair fell over his forehead and this time he didn't bother to brush it back. His mouth was a thin, stern line, his face losing its puckish illusion of youthfulness as his expression became absorbed . . . intent.

Rosalind's skin prickled with self-awareness under the rough towelling. She was suddenly conscious that she was lying there, to all intents and purposes helpless, nude beneath her robe, while Luke bent over her, fully dressed. There was something uncomfortably erotic about the situation—a purely atavistic feminine response to the threat of male dominance.

Not that Luke was any worry to her in that direction, she told herself hurriedly, but she wondered at her own waywardness. Ever since her disaster with Justin she had preferred to be the controlling partner in her relationships with men. Even in her secret fantasies she had never felt excited by the idea of being sexually dominated, of being held captive by passion and aroused against her will by a skilful seducer . . . she was immune to the appeal of dashing sheikhs and silken bindings. So why such thoughts should sneak into her mind now, when she was feeling so thoroughly ghastly and totally unattractive, was difficult to comprehend.

She wondered exactly what was going through Luke's mind. Nothing as wildly inappropriate as what was going through her own, she decided as she watched the shift of his expression. What ever made her think that he was young for his age? Right now he looked every one of his twenty-eight years—and more... disconcertingly mature and sombre in his seriousness.

His eyes had that glaze of absent-minded, see-nothing vagueness which Rosalind was coming to realise indicated a see-all state of mind. He was focusing on the big picture rather than on the one immediately in front of him, his brain adding up all the possibilities and cross-referencing them with what information he already had.

'Do you mean it's some form of motion sickness?' he asked puzzled. 'But how can that be...? You weren't sick on the flight.'

'Oh, for goodness sake! Not *motion—morning*,' she stressed weakly, realising that he wasn't going to give up until he had a satisfactory answer. 'Look, just pass me over one of those crackers just there on the bedside table and then toddle downstairs and make me a cup of tea... weak, with just a little milk and not too hot—'

'Morning? What do you—? *Morning sickness!*' He jackknifed upright again, setting up an unpleasant vibration in the mattress. 'My God, do you mean—you're *pregnant*?'

'For God's sake, stop rocking the boat and pass me the damned cracker!' moaned Rosalind, wishing she were well enough to enjoy his shocked reaction.

'Pregnant!' he repeated, doing as he was bid, his face almost as pale as hers under the natural tan as he stood uncertainly next to the bed. 'Who's the father?' he asked abruptly.

'Jordan... my brother-in-law,' said Rosalind, munching experimentally.

'*What*?' If she had thought he looked devilish before, now he was Satan, King of Hell, come to fry her for every sin she had ever dreamed of committing. 'You've been having an affair with your own sister's *husband*?'

he thundered accusingly, smoke practically pouring from his pinched nostrils.

'No, of course not!' she cried, stuffing the rest of the cracker in her mouth with kill-or-cure haste. Jordan would hit the roof if *that* rumour ever got around! 'Jordan's the father, but of *Olivia's*—my sister's—baby!'

His eyes went darkly opaque. 'My God,' he breathed. 'Are you acting as a surrogate mother—is that it? Are you carrying their child implanted in your womb because your sister can't carry a full-term pregnancy?'

His leap of imagination took her breath away. She was glad that she was already lying down. It wasn't often these days that she was taken so spectacularly off guard. She felt a deep, dangerous stirring of dark emotions which she ruthlessly repressed.

'*No*! Honestly, Luke, I don't know where you get such wild ideas from; you're as bad as the tabloids—' She bit her lip, hoping he hadn't noticed the slip. The cracker miraculously seemed to have settled down in comfortable residence and she pushed herself cautiously up against the pillows and took pity on his confusion.

'I'm not carrying *anyone's* child, OK? I'm not pregnant at all; I just have the symptoms.' She thumped the mattress with a frustrated fist and threatened fiercely, 'Oh, I'm going to *kill* her for doing this to me when I get back home!'

Sharp alarm briefly pierced the bewildered dark eyes. 'Kill who?' he said sharply.

'Olivia, my sister, that's who!' She braced herself for the usual scepticism as she attempted to explain as succinctly as possible, '*Olivia's* the one who's pregnant, not me. We're twins, you see, and we've always shared a really close mental and physical connection. When we were children, whenever Olivia got ill I did too... or I showed all the symptoms but not the illness... and vice versa. Fortunately it's faded quite a bit as we've grown older and become more separate in our lives. Sometimes it's just the echo of sympathetic feeling, a not-quite-rightness, but sometimes it's a real, rip-roaring snorter!'

'Like now.'

Strangers rarely took her affinity with her twin seriously and Rosalind's mouth formed a pink O at his apparently easy acceptance of the bizarre truth. But then, she reasoned, it was no more bizarre than *his* guess.

'Like now,' she conceded ruefully. She sat up further, and brightened as she realised the nausea had passed. She felt perfectly normal again. She grinned her relief. 'But, hey, it's just a temporary condition and it's not usually this drastic—at least not for me. Jordan told me it's far worse for poor Olivia, who throws up on and off for *hours* every single morning—and she hates being ill and helpless even more than I do!'

Thirty minutes later, at the balcony restaurant, Luke was watching in appalled fascination as she poured more syrup onto the plate of waffles next to her decimated serving of bacon, eggs, grilled tomato and hash browns.

'I don't know how you can do that,' he murmured, shuddering as she took a dreamy bite of the sticky-sweet concoction. 'Anyone else would have settled for dry toast.'

'I have a naturally high tolerance for food,' she grinned, paraphrasing his words from last night as she cast a disparaging look at his orange juice and the plain wholemeal toast that had followed his bowl of cereal and fruit. 'I think it's something to do with my body chemistry. And don't forget that Olivia's hormones are busily informing me that I'm now eating for two!'

'You'll have to make sure you start getting a bit of exercise today. You don't burn up many calories sunbathing.'

'Exactly my plan.' Rosalind's smug grin made him eye her warily. He was beginning to know the look that bespoke mischief. 'When we've finished eating we'll go downstairs and book our jet-skis. I hope we're still early enough to get a couple for this morning.'

He put down his orange juice. *'Jet-skis!'*

'They rent them out by the half-hour but I say we get them for a full hour. Surely you didn't think that we were just going to sit around and flirt with each other all day, did you, Luke?' she said sweetly, enjoying his startled consternation. 'That wouldn't burn up very many calories either. Flirting isn't a passive art, you know; it's as much physical as verbal. Being able to flirt on the wing, so to speak, increases your chances of success ... Besides, if you do interesting things you set up opportunities to meet a more interesting type of woman. I take it you haven't ridden a jet-ski before.'

'No, nor ever wanted to,' he said, glancing down at the short jetty and pontoons which marked off the area of the beach which had been set aside for the safe use of power boats and jet-skis. 'Can't we do something less ... noisy?'

'No, we can't.' She ruthlessly brushed aside his objection. 'I thought you said you didn't want to encroach on my holiday? Well, if we do things my way we'll both get what we want—I'll have some fun and you'll provide yourself with a stimulating new experience to talk about.

'Trust me—once you get the hang of it you'll love it,' she predicted, polishing off another waffle. Her green eyes shimmered with innocence as she leaned over the table to add in a low purr that made a flush streak across his cheekbones, 'Just think of the pleasure of having all that throbbing power between your legs. Who knows? It might prompt you to discover a totally new aspect of your personality!'

But it was Rosalind who was first to make that discovery a short time later as she prowled restlessly around Luke's chalet while she waited for him to change into his swimsuit and collect his beach gear. They were only going to have a short wait for their jet-skis and she didn't want to waste a minute of their allocated time. Since she was wearing a matching bikini under her sunflower-printed cotton Lycra swing-dress she had only needed to slip next door and fetch her beach bag, give her teeth a quick clean and slap on some sunscreen. Typically, Luke was obviously being more meticulous . . . or merely reinforcing his mistrust of her interpretation of fun.

Impatient with the wait and incurably nosy, Rosalind couldn't resist poking around his tidily arranged possessions to see what they revealed about his personality . . . other than the fact that he was a relentless neatnik. She was investigating his reading matter, noting the depressing lack of holiday trash amongst the pile on the small teak table, when she came across the torn-out pages of a magazine. It was the article about her that she had read on the flight from New Zealand, the story that rehashed the worst excesses of her 'wild child' exploits, carefully undated so that an uninformed reader might assume they had occurred weeks rather than years ago.

Luke must have torn it out of his copy of the magazine on the plane. Her heart began to thump as she realised the implications.

Rosalind was still staring at the crumpled pages when Luke came down the stairs, dressed as he had been before, except for the dark shadow of his swim-shorts showing under the white trousers and the sunglasses hanging out of his shirt pocket.

He halted abruptly when he saw what she had in her hand, his mouth closing over what he had been going to say, and Rosalind was stung by a sense of betrayal.

'You knew!' she attacked him, snapping her fist closed and balling up the offending paper with vicious, jerky movements of her fingers. 'Damn it—you read this and you knew who I was even before I sat down beside you on that first flight, didn't you? *Didn't you?*'

He shrugged, his eyes faintly hooded under the etched brows, his narrow face revealing nothing of what was going through his mind. And she had thought that he was so wonderfully transparent...had convinced herself that his air of bumbling helplessness was cute as well as harmless!

'Well, answer me, damn it!' she hissed at him, goaded by his silence, golden sunflowers flaring out around her slender hips as she stormed closer to impale him with the emerald fury of her eyes. God forbid that he should turn out to be a journalist after all.

'Why didn't you say you'd recognised me?' she demanded, spoiling for a reply that would allow her temper full rein.

But instead of looking guilty Luke casually bent over and picked up a white panama hat from a rattan chair, holding it loosely alongside his thigh as he answered. 'Because I received the very strong impression that you were travelling incognito, wanting to avoid drawing any attention to yourself or your identity,' he said, with the calmness of sincerity. 'Was I so wrong?'

'Well, no,' she admitted, unwilling to let go of her anger, or face the underlying emotion which had prompted her to lash out. 'But you still could have given me *some* indication—'

'How—without intruding on the privacy which was obviously so vital that you went to the trouble of disguising yourself?' he asked, with devastating logic.

She brooded on that one. He had managed to turn the tables very neatly, but that didn't mean that he was exonerated.

'What about later, when I told you I was an actress and you said you didn't go to the theatre? You could have mentioned the article; you didn't have to *still* pretend you didn't know anything about me,' she insisted sharply, the strong sense of pique she had felt at the time still mockingly clear in her memory.

'Ah...well, perhaps I couldn't help teasing you a little bit there—'

'Hah!'

He ignored the accusing sound. 'But by then it would have been awkward to admit otherwise without causing embarrassment,' he continued evenly. 'I thought it more diplomatic to behave as if we were strangers, which to all intents and purposes we still are...'

Rosalind's chin went up in a familiar gesture of dramatic defiance. '*I* wouldn't have been embarrassed!' she declared, her eyes blazing with the refusal to apologise for the way that she had lived. She had made mistakes, but she had paid the price for them too, and in one case would go *on* paying, for the rest of her life...

'Maybe not, but *I* would.' He made a self-deprecating gesture with his hands. 'I thought you might think I had done it with malice aforethought—pretending not to recognise you in order to scrape an acquaintance, so that I could boost my ego by boasting about our conversation later...selling my story, that kind of thing. I know there are some people like that...'

He looked down at the hat in his hand, sliding the brim between his fingers with his other hand. 'And I didn't think that particular story was something you would want to discuss, particularly with a stranger. Unless you brought up the subject yourself, I didn't see a way to mention it...'

'Hmm.' Rosalind summoned up her worst-case scenario to attack his aura of guilty innocence. 'So you're not in some kind of security intelligence service?'

His head jerked up. 'No!'

'Or a detective?'

He shook his head, the movement blurring the expression in the dark eyes.

'A reporter?'

'God forbid!' he blurted out.

He was either being honest or he was a spectacularly good liar. Rosalind only had her instincts to go on.

'Hmm.' She tapped her foot, reluctant to let him entirely off the hook as she tried to think whether there were any other unwelcome possibilities she hadn't covered.

'You needn't worry about your privacy being compromised,' he said, as if reading her scurrying thoughts. 'Accountants are, by the very nature of their work, trustworthy and discreet. We're often privy to extremely sensitive, private information about people's lives and we'd soon find ourselves out of work if we boasted about our inside knowledge. Not that I'm one for boasting anyway...'

Rosalind immediately felt like a paranoid witch. Of course he wasn't, and that was part of the reason why he couldn't hold a woman's interest beyond the first ten minutes!

'There's nothing very private about *my* life at the moment!' She threw the ball of magazine pages at his chest, amazed at the speed of his reflexes when his hand snapped out and caught it before it hit him. 'I hope you don't believe everything you read in that kind of publication!'

'I prefer to form my own opinions.'

'So? Aren't you even going to ask me how much of that trash is true?' she taunted. 'Don't you want to know all the gory little details that the story left out?'

'Only if you want to tell me,' he said, with just the right touch of open-minded disinterest.

She wondered whether he expected his diffidence to result in a burst of confidence. She tossed her head. 'I don't!'

He passed the test with flying colours.

'In that case shall we go and try out those damned noise-making machines you booked?' he said, settling his hat on his head and indicating the door.

'Why on earth did you tear out the damned article anyway?' she brooded moments later as they skirted a fallen coconut on the path.

'Impulse...I suppose as a kind of souvenir of our meeting.'

'You don't ask for much class in your souvenirs, do you?'

'You mean like toothpicks and coffee-sachets have class?' he shot back smoothly, making her laugh.

They cut down to the beach and strolled along the satiny sand towards the jetty, skirting the early sun-bathers and the odd child with a bucket and spade. Families with teenagers rather than young children or babies seemed to be predominant at the Palms, for which Rosalind was quietly thankful.

After they had picked up a couple of towels from the hotel's beach kiosk Rosalind veered towards the water's edge, hopping along as she removed her canvas slip-ons so that she could swish through the gently lapping waves. Without a word Luke took possession of her drawstring bag, paralleling her on the firm sand just above the waterline, keeping his beach sandals meticulously dry. The tide was fully in, the water so clear that Rosalind could see the rocks and pieces of dead coral dotting the sandy seabed as it sloped gently away from the wide beach.

The sun was already hot, beating down on her wide-brimmed straw sunhat, making her glad of its shade mantling her shoulders, which were left bare by her halter-necked dress and bikini. There was a slight breeze—just enough to stir the palm leaves fringing the beach and gently billow out the sail of a windsurfer sketching a lazy progress across the glittering plane of the water. They would do that next, Rosalind decided, admiring the skill of the briefly clad male as he deftly changed the direction of his board.

A sea-bird wheeled overhead and further out towards the line of yachts moored across the bay a pair of snorkels broke the surface. It was a picture-perfect moment and Rosalind took a deep breath, happy to be alive.

She placed a hand on the top of her hat and gave a small skip, enjoying the feel of the silky water creaming around her ankles and the spray of lukewarm droplets smattering up over her thighs and the flirty hem of her mini-dress. She was aware of Luke's easy, loose-limbed stride matching her brief burst of speed and glanced over to catch his eyes on her shaded face.

The white hat suited his olive complexion, she mused, and, tilted as it was on a slight angle, managed to give his face a rakish look that most women would find intriguing. In fact, each time she saw him Rosalind was obliged to reassess her opinion of his potential.

'No more ill effects from this morning?' he said quickly, as if to forestall any comment on his watchfulness.

But Rosalind was used to being stared at and she merely shook her head with a rueful grin. 'Not me. Poor Olivia is probably still hung over a bowl, though. Even anti-nausea medication doesn't work; at least, not in the recommended doses. If Jordan could buy her way out of morning sickness I think he'd be prepared to spend the entire Pendragon family fortune!'

He removed his aviator sunglasses from his pocket and slipped them on, hiding his eyes. 'I hope not, since my livelihood depends on it.'

Rosalind was deceived by the casualness of his revelation. 'What do you mean?'

'I happen to work for his cousin, William.'

Rosalind nearly fell on her face in the water in mid-skip. 'You work for *Will*—?' she screeched inelegantly. Rosalind had dated Jordan's cousin a couple of times but purely on a friendly welcome-to-the-family basis, for he was a businessman to his fingertips, far too conservative for her taste, and she had been too *outré* for his.

Luke's stride didn't falter. 'For the Pendragon Corporation, yes.'

Rosalind was blown away by the coincidence. She splashed out of the water to trot after him on sandy feet. 'Where?'

'In Wellington.'

She shrugged off a frisson of unpleasant memory at the mention of the city. 'I didn't mean geographically. I meant—doing what?'

'I coordinate the preparation of various company accounts for taxation purposes.'

Taxes. She might have known!

'I can't get over what an incredible coincidence this is—my sister is married to your boss's cousin!' she said as she waved to the young Malaysian up at the marine centre from whom she had hired the jet-skis and followed his pointing finger to the gleaming red and white machines being held in knee-deep water by another employee. 'Why, that makes us practically *family*!' She laughed, halting beneath a tall coconut palm that slanted out over the beach.

Luke spread out his towel in the shade of the fronds, carefully placing her bag on top of it. 'I wouldn't go quite that far.'

'Well, kissing cousins at the very least.' She gave him a sultry smile of sly mischief and tossed her hat down beside her bag. She tugged up the hem of her stretchy cotton Lycra dress and whipped it over her head. 'You should have mentioned the connection sooner, then I wouldn't have been so suspicious of you,' she said, amused by his half-step backwards at her sudden strip.

For a moment it seemed as if he wouldn't answer. In the black lenses of his sunglasses she could see twin images of herself reflected—slim, laughing figures in yellow floral bikinis that covered only the bare essentials.

Luke found his voice. 'I thought it might sound encroaching,' he murmured.

She planted one hand on the delicate arch of her hip and shook an exasperated finger at him. 'Luke James, you are the *least* encroaching man I have ever met! Stop worrying about what people might think and start taking a few chances. Now, get your gear off and let me show you how to give a woman a good time!'

He flushed, his jaw clenching, but he did what he was bid. His naked torso had perfect triangular proportions—strongly defined shoulders and compact, hairless chest tapering to a washboard abdomen and narrow waist. His hips and legs were as whipcord-lean as the rest of him.

She whistled at him to show that she was impressed, then chuckled as she led him down to the water, wading in to say to the man holding the jet-skis, 'We just want one for the first ten minutes or so.' She jerked her thumb over her shoulder. 'Luke's never ridden one before, so I'll take him out on the back of mine so he can see how it's done.'

'O.K. Did you read the rules at the centre?'

Rosalind nodded and he quickly reiterated the main ones and gave her a brief tour of the controls as she pulled herself up to straddle the red padded seat.

Luke hung back when Rosalind indicated for him to mount up behind her.

'Come on; time is money, as you accountants would say. This is a two-seater, see?' she said, scooting forward to show him there was ample room.

He still hesitated. 'If you drive as recklessly as you seem to do everything else I hope the hotel has adequate insurance.'

Her green eyes flared at the insult but she held onto her temper, telling herself he was merely being his usual cautious self. 'I promise you won't get hurt...the worst that can happen is that we'll both get wet. And this guy will come out in his Zodiac if the engine conks out.'

Her condescending tone and the glance of amused tolerance she exchanged with the hotel employee was impetus enough. With a grim smile Luke swung up into the seat.

'You can hang onto the handholds at the side or me—whichever feels more secure,' Rosalind yelled as she turned the key in the ignition and the engine roared to life. The front of the craft lifted as she gunned the throttle and they leapt forward to crest the swell of the incoming waves.

She could hear Luke's faint groans as they plunged from wave to wave; then they were out in the calm of deeper waters and after a few fancy turns and sharp, sweeping swathes she felt his hands snap around her waist. She laughed. She had known he wouldn't be able to keep his distance for long. For one thing hunching down to the handholds was uncomfortable for any length of time if you were above average height.

'If that's your idea of fun, I think I can do without it,' he said acidly when Rosalind finally sped back in and throttled down beside the other jet-ski.

'It's always uncomfortable riding pillion because you know you don't have any control over what's happening. Once you have the handlebars to grip onto you'll find it's quite a different feeling.' She grinned as he dropped into the waist-deep water. 'Did you see how I worked the throttle, or do you want it explained again?'

He placed a hand on the seat of the other jet-ski and vaulted onto it in a single, fluid movement. 'It seems to be not much different from riding a motorcycle.'

'You've ridden a motorcycle?' Rosalind blinked tangled wet lashes at a brief, shocking image of that lean, hard body encased in sexy black leathers insolently unzipped from throat to groin.

He seemed unreasonably irritated by her surprise. 'I owned one as a teenager,' he flung at her. 'A Harley, as a matter of fact. You don't have to be born to be wild like you to enjoy the occasional walk on the wild side, Roz!'

And with that he took off in a shower of spray, handling the powerful machine with only a slight clumsiness which vanished as soon as he hit the first wave, rising to his feet to absorb the impact of landing and leaning straight into a superbly flashy turn. Rosalind's gaping mouth closed as her ready sense of humour rescued her from the uncomfortable physical awareness of a few moments ago and she roared after him with a rebel yell of delight. Talk about being a fast learner! At this rate she was going to have trouble keeping pace with her protegé!

# CHAPTER SIX

LUKE provided her with delightful sport for the next hour as they raced back and forth across the bay, circling the buoys and pontoons, taking it in turns to ride each other's wake and duelling with other jet-skis who dared challenge for supremacy of the waves.

It was the first time Rosalind had seen him completely uninhibited and she was startled by the streak of fierce competitiveness he revealed in their games. He liked to win, and when he did made no bones about enjoying his victory, punching a fist to the sky, his triumphant laugh ringing out over the water. She couldn't quite believe that it was the same man who would hardly say boo to a goose on dry land!

Even more surprisingly, Rosalind was the one to flag first. When their time was finally up she was glad to hand over her jet-ski to someone else and stagger up the beach, cheerfully admitting as she flopped down on her towel that her arms and legs felt like jelly from the constant strain of controlling all that horsepower.

'Not to mention another part of my anatomy that's taken a pounding,' she groaned as she wriggled on her back to make a nice contoured hollow in the sand for the tender region and propped her hat against the top of her head so that it shaded her face. 'I must have lost more condition than I thought on that wretched island!'

Luke, who seemed if anything to be *more* energised by the experience, shook his towel before settling down beside her, leaning back on braced arms, his knees drawn up in front of him, flicking his wet hair back with a sharp toss of his head.

'Are you talking about the film you've just finished?' His curiosity was no longer constrained by having to pretend ignorance of her background.

Rosalind pulled a wry face. 'You mean which almost finished *me*.'

She embarked on her humorously harrowing tale of woman-eating sharks, broken bones and mosquitoes the size of vampire bats. 'It was the sheer *incompetency* of the whole thing that I found so infuriating,' she finished, with an angry twist to her mobile mouth. 'I wouldn't have minded the deprivations so much if it had been a cracking script, but by the time the director had done a million rewrites the characters were practically incomprehensible. As a break into films it was *not* a good career move...'

'I thought you preferred the stage anyway,' he said, confirming that he had read the small print of the article, not just the trashy bits. 'What made you want to do *this* film?'

She sighed. He had an instinct for innocently framing awkward questions.

'Impulse. I was looking to expand my horizons. The original script was actually quite good...and the director begged me to!' She opened her eyes and found him regarding her thoughtfully. She moved her expressive hands restlessly. 'Trina was a friend of mine. Hell, I didn't know that since we left drama school she'd only done commercials and music videos!'

'You didn't think to check out her credentials before you committed yourself?' It was the accountant not the jet-ski speed pirate talking, and his incredulous tone put her on the defensive.

'I told you, she was an old friend. I liked her. It was a loyalty thing.'

'Misplaced loyalty as it turned out.'

Rosalind bristled at the hint of contempt. 'Yes, well, that's the whole point of loyalty, isn't it—sticking with people through the bad as well as the good? Trina did her best; her ambition simply overreached her abilities. At least she was willing to take the risk and try, and I respect her for *that*.'

His raised eyebrow was a taunt in itself and she thought that if he had been a calculating man she would have suspected him of playing the devil's advocate purely to provoke her impulsive retort. 'Maybe it was the element of risk that attracted you to the project in the first place.'

'Maybe it was,' she prevaricated. 'But at least I came out of it with a minimum wage. The investors must have taken a bath!'

As she'd suspected, the financial red herring was too tempting for him to resist, and they discussed the intricacies of film financing before Rosalind managed gradually to edge the conversation around to a subject of potentially greater interest—Luke's Harley-Davidson-owning days. However, they turned out to be disappointingly tame...a case of riding the motorcycle back and forth to university and to his part-time job. He had never even belonged to a motorcycle club, let alone a gang. As far as he was concerned, his grunt-machine had been merely a convenient and economical form of transport, with the added advantage of being a classic which would appreciate in value and therefore could be viewed in the light of an investment.

'A conformist without a cause!' Rosalind murmured, wistfully relinquishing the illicit vision of a leather-clad Luke lounging astride a sexy hunk of chrome and black, a cigarette and a sneer dangling from his lips.

She delved to find a replacement image but it was tough going trying to get Luke to open up about himself. On general subjects he was capable of being provoked into something bordering on eloquence but when it came to the personal stuff he retreated into his awkward shell.

She did manage to patch together the picture of an orphaned only child who became an adopted only child,

then a conscientious student who had set himself a series
of goals towards which he had worked with relentless
dedication. Not for him the usual wild student friv-
olities. He had lived at home and, while his adoptive
parents had been comfortably well off and prepared to
pay generously for his education, they'd believed strongly
in the work ethic, so that Luke had had to work at a
variety of jobs while he was studying, to help ease the
burden of his keep. Rosalind lazily admitted that since
she was old enough to do walk-ons she had only ever
worked in the theatre.

'And loved every minute of it,' she sighed. 'Up until
now, anyway.'

She bit her lip as the self-pitying words slipped out,
and Luke rolled onto his side, propping his temple on
a loose fist. 'What's so different now?'

Rosalind looked straight up at the cloudless sky. Her
mouth went dry at the thought of saying it...as dry as
it had felt the last few times she'd been on stage, in those
awful moments when her mind had gone totally blank,
so that she hadn't even been able to remember what play
she was in, let alone what her next lines were. All she
had been conscious of was those eyes trained on her from
the darkened auditorium—the eyes of friends, fans,
strangers—and one stranger in particular who might be
out there, watching, waiting for a word or gesture or a
look which his psychosis could interpret as an invitation
to fulfil his frightening fantasies...

'Oh, just a slight crisis of confidence. I'll get over it,'
she forced herself to say lightly, with more optimism than
she felt.

'Did you say confidence or conscience?'

She turned her head sharply. In spite of the increasing
heat he hadn't replaced his hat or sunglasses, but the
palm fronds stirring overhead dappled his sun-burnished
face with fluttering shadows that made his expression
difficult to read.

'*Confidence,*' she articulated, deciding to give him the benefit of the doubt. Perhaps he still had water in his ears. 'I was talking about my *stage* confidence. When you're out there in front of an audience you have to be able to submerge yourself in the role. Once you start letting other things intrude you're in trouble. And worrying about whether you're going to have a panic attack in the middle of a performance can become a self-fulfilling prophecy—'

She broke off. She hadn't meant to reveal so much. She hadn't even spoken of her career concerns to her twin. She was tough, determined, a seasoned professional. She had expected to bounce back from adversity with her customary swift resilience. But what if she didn't?

She rolled over onto her stomach, burying her face in her folded arms to conceal the fleeting self-doubt which might be evident on her expressive features. She forced herself back into the role of carefree companion, her voice muffled as she said lightly, 'Speaking of confidence, you seemed to have plenty out there on the water. Now you've got to build on that image.

'The time-honoured ploy of the beach flirt is offering to rub sunscreen onto a woman's back. It gives you the chance to sound sexy *and* caring, and if she accepts then you can practically guarantee she's interested. But don't make the mistake of groping. The first time should be sensuous yet brisk. Your aim is to show her you're a man she can trust...'

There was a silence, several heartbeats long.

'Are you asking me to apply your sunscreen for you?' he said, in a distinctly edgy tone.

Rosalind grinned into her towel, her spirits revived. 'Well, I'm sure you need the practice and I'm prepared to sacrifice myself for the greater good of womankind,' she mocked. 'I'll even give you a critique when you're done! For a start you could show some enthusiasm. Try and sound eager to get your hands on my body...'

'Does your throat count?' he delighted her by muttering.

She turned her head to the side and, sure enough, found his eyes on the tender sweep of her neck, exposed in all its delicate vulnerability by her pixie haircut. 'Why, Luke, do you harbour erotic fantasies about being a vampire?'

His colour had darkened, although it could have been the heat of the sun on his bare head that was making him look flushed. 'I was thinking of strangling rather than biting!' he growled, reluctantly picking up the tube of sunscreen that was poking out of the top of her beach bag.

'Pity. Vampires are much sexier than common-or-garden stranglers!'

His subsequent wordless application of the sunscreen was far more brisk than sensuous but Rosalind didn't take him to task because she discovered the sensation of those firm hands massaging across her sun-warmed skin too disturbing for comfort. This time there was nothing to blame for the faint buzz that vibrated through her nerve-ends but her own bio-electrical system. Wherever Luke touched her it was as if a static discharge occurred—one that seemed to grow rather than to fade with continued contact. Rosalind was literally live to his touch!

Her amusement was mixed with chagrin at the unexpected physical attraction, especially as Luke gave no sign of being similarly affected. He was supposed to be an entertaining holiday distraction, not an added complication to her life. Still, as long as she kept that firmly in the forefront of her mind there could be no danger of her behaving like a real-life Pygmalion and falling in love with her own creation. She had made a promise to Luke, and she couldn't let him down. She would shake him up and turn him loose and in the meantime rely on her strong self-discipline to control any inconvenient pangs of lust!

So from then on Rosalind threw herself whole-heartedly into the task of making Luke seem irresistible to members of the opposite sex while quietly maintaining a discreet physical distance herself. She deliberately gave him no rest, filling every moment with activities which she hoped would so focus his concentration that he would forget the awkward self-consciousness that seemed to afflict him around other people.

Following their jet-skiing success, Rosalind took him snorkelling later the same afternoon and was relieved to find that he was as sleek as a seal in the water, though he regrettably seemed more interested in the teeming marine life on the reef than in the occasional eligible human female who drifted in his direction. They joined a dozen or so others in one of Tioman's distinctive, long wooden bumboats which plied for hire around the coast, to travel to a tiny, rocky off-shore island a scant few minutes from the hotel jetty.

Rosalind marvelled at the vivid fans of waving coral, and the iridescent colours of some of the fish that darted in and out of the rocks. There were gliding mantas and creeping crustaceans, flowing sea anemones and rocking sea urchins with jewel-like blue spots glowing between their long spines.

As they floated face down in the shallows around the island Rosalind was tempted by the idea of booking a scuba-dive and exploring the deeper riches of the sea, until Luke drew closer to her side and motioned towards the seabed, pointing out a young shark sleeking between the rocks. She decided then that perhaps she wasn't ready yet for another close encounter with any denizens of the deep!

The next day they took a three-hour guided walk through the forested valleys to the village of Juara, on the other side of the island. It was hot and still in the depths of the interior, the trunks of massive trees bearing such evocative names as sandalwood and camphor soaring skywards from the forest floor, their distant green canopy almost obscured by the lacy foliage of the palms and shrubs of the undergrowth through which they walked, and Rosalind was grateful to their guide for his frequent pauses on the banks of cool, boulder-strewn streams.

The steamy heat seemed to have little effect on Luke, who chafed at Rosalind's tendency to fall back amongst the stragglers and linger over every new orchid spike, every small lizard or exotic butterfly she spied.

In the afternoon they caught a bumboat back around the south coast, stopping off at Mukut village, from which they trekked up to the famous waterfall. Luke had never seen *South Pacific* and had been slightly contemptuous of the reason for Rosalind's eager pilgrimage, but he couldn't deny that the scenery itself was spectacular and Rosalind had her revenge for his sarcastic remarks about cultural imperialism in general and the silliness of musicals in particular by singing him every song from the show that she could remember, much to the amusement of others they passed on the walk.

Washing men out of her hair seemed particularly appealing, and she sang that one several times with special emphasis on their way back down to the boat, accompanying it with jaunty dance steps that criss-crossed in front of Luke's stride until he was goaded into begging her to stop.

Luke got his own back the next day, however, when Rosalind offered to teach him to windsurf. When he appeared ready to protest she overrode him with her usual bossy enthusiasm, stressing that everyone was clumsy at first but it was just a matter of persistence. She very kindly didn't say that she expected him to be a more clumsy beginner than most, but the message was subtly delivered by her condescending grin. And so it proved.

She made Luke walk parallel to her on the sand while she sailed the board along to the secluded end of the long beach to show him how it was done. The breeze was gentle but steady and the sea glass-like in its smoothness, so the conditions were as perfect as they could be for a beginner.

Given Luke's seal-like grace in the water, Rosalind was confident that once he got over his nervous fear of making a fool of himself he would soon pick up the basics, but to her frustration he proved so fumblingly inept that it took her ages merely to get him standing upright on the board. In the process she became his waterlogged sea anchor, her arms and hands aching from holding the board steady while he tried to find his elusive sense of balance.

When, finally, after more than an hour of careful coaching, he progressed to actually pulling the sail upright, he would invariably lose his stability before the wind had time to fill it and topple off again, usually in her direction, smacking down in a tangle of splayed limbs, sending yet another shock blast of salt water shooting up into her eyes, nose and mouth.

She couldn't lose her temper because each time it happened Luke was so very apologetic, so desperate to master the simple skill, so insistent that if she would just bear with him he would eventually succeed. She didn't have the heart to tell him that he might as well give it up as a lost cause, not after she had stressed the importance of persistence.

Even worse, his body seemed to be constantly bumping and rubbing up against hers as they struggled with the board and the wet sail. She had to help boost him up onto the deck and guide his legs into position and reach around him to show him the handholds. Every time she moved, his cool flesh somehow got in her way. Her hands slipped and slid against his smooth, wet skin, sometimes skidding off into dangerous territory, and the water proved a wonderful conductor for the zinging electrical awareness that intensified each time their bodies made contact.

Oh, for the temperate waters of New Zealand where most windsurfers wore demure wetsuits! Rosalind inwardly wailed as Luke took another tumble, one slick thigh fleetingly thrust between hers, its slight roughness rasping the highly sensitive skin and catching on the silky fabric of her bikini, giving it an intimate little nudge that, for Rosalind, was the last straw.

She faked, very professionally, standing on something sharp and painful. Just painful enough to necessitate her limping ashore to check the wound, not painful enough to require his assistance.

'It's not as if there's any blood. I'll be fine... you carry on with what you're doing,' she said, hastily wading beyond his long reach. 'Maybe you just need a bit of time fooling about on your own to get the hang of it, anyway...'

She limped up the beach to their towels in a masterful piece of underplaying, conscious of Luke's eyes boring into her back. She sat down and made a show of inspecting the sole of her foot before giving him a reassuring wave and relaxing back on her elbows with a grateful sigh. She watched him broodingly. This was ridiculous. Why was she running away? He was a perfectly nice man. Why on earth *shouldn't* she conduct this phony flirtation for real?

Her eyes drifted closed as she contemplated the idea. Although Luke might be inexperienced with women he was intellectually mature, a full-grown, well-educated adult holding down a highly responsible job. It wouldn't be as if she were seducing an innocent boy for her own amusement. And there would be no question of exploring the attraction if it didn't prove to be mutual...

She must have dozed off because when next she opened her eyes Luke was nowhere in sight. She sat up in alarm, her anxious gaze sweeping the bay, visions of finding him floating face down in the water dancing in her head. And it would be all her fault for pushing him beyond his physical capabilities!

Her jaw dropped when she finally spotted the distinctive green sail emblazoned with the hotel's palm logo breezing out towards the open sea. As she watched, Luke shifted his weight, swinging the sail around and moving back towards the shore, tacking to take best advantage of the light off-shore wind.

Hmm!

By the time he beached the board and strolled up the sand her suspicions were simmering.

'That was a pretty good run for an absolute beginner.'

He picked up his towel and mopped down his body with distracting thoroughness. 'Actually you were right—it was a lot easier without you there pointing out every mistake and making me nervous.' His face disappeared into the towel as he rubbed his hair.

'Oh, really?' she drawled, relaxing back on her elbows, dipping her head so that the straw brim of her hat concealed her study of the way the concave plane of his stomach flexed with his movements.

'Yes, once you figure out how to stay upright the rest just seems to fall into place!'

Her suspicions were unappeased by his muffled words. 'Luke James, is that the first time you've been windsurfing?'

His face emerged from the folds of the towel. 'Surely you should have asked me that question before we started? How's the foot?'

'Fine,' she said absently, trying to figure out whether his answer constituted a confession of exaggerated ineptitude.

'Is it? May I see?'

Before she realised what he was doing he had dropped to his knees in front of her feet, his buttocks resting on his heels, his fingers gripping her ankle.

'No!'

She tried to jerk away but his fingers tightened around the bone as he lifted her foot for inspection.

'Don't worry, I won't hurt you,' he murmured, brushing the grains of sand gently off her sole with the thumb of his free hand.

'I told you, it was nothing,' she said breathlessly as he frowned, bending closer to the site, his damp hair fanning forward around the widow's peak, his thumb moving in another probing caress. His nail scraped lightly across her skin and her toes curled involuntarily towards the ball of her foot, a husky sound of protest issuing from her throat. He paused, his lids flicking up in instant enquiry.

'I'm ticklish.' Unbelievably she could feel her face pinken at the husky lie. She, the mistress of the mask, whose whole professional training had been aimed at the weaving of believable lies. She *never* blushed...except when it was written in the stage directions!

'I'll be careful.' His lids sank down again and Rosalind braced herself to have her silly deception exposed. 'I don't see— Ah, wait a moment, what's this...?' His short thumbnail dug into the soft, resilient pad of flesh. 'It looks like...it could be a shell splinter, or some sort of spine...'

'Could it?' Rosalind hadn't really looked closely at her foot, knowing there was nothing there to see. 'Uh...it's not hurting now—'

'Did you feel a stinging or burning sensation when it happened?'

'Neither,' she said truthfully. But she could certainly feel something now! She wished he would stop rubbing his thumb back and forth like that; it was sending tingles of sensation shooting up the insides of her calves and thighs.

A heat that had nothing to do with the sun pooled in her stomach. Her fingers dug into the sand at her sides and her free leg shifted restlessly, drawing up slightly to hide the vulnerable triangle at the apex of her thighs. She could feel her nipples begin to firm and knew they would soon be evident through the thin, shiny fabric of her hot-pink bikini.

'Whatever it is I don't think we should leave it in there, do you?' he said gravely. 'In this climate infections can set in very quickly if you ignore a wound...'

'Unfortunately I don't happen to have a needle on me,' joked Rosalind weakly, patting her bare sides. She regretted her mistake immediately as his eyes accepted the licence to rove. A quick glance down confirmed that he couldn't fail to notice the explicit outline of her breasts, the smooth swells, gathered and lifted by the halter-neck of her bikini, projecting the stiff little crowns forward into stark prominence. And she couldn't even blame it on the chill of the water!

His gaze took on a familiar blank, unfocused intensity as it rose to her face, his fingers tightening on her ankle as she instinctively tried again to twist it free.

'We'll just have to improvise, then...' he murmured. And, still holding her gaze, he bent his head, shifting his grip to cup her heel, tilting her foot delicately aslant with his other hand as he placed it against his open mouth. Rosalind gasped as she felt his teeth sink deep into the tender pad of her sole and a hot, wet suction begin a rhythmic tugging at her flesh.

'Luke!' Her exclamation of shocked protest was undermined by the insidious weakness that flooded through her body. Her elbows collapsed and her shoulderblades hit the sand, her hat rolling off her bright head, leaving her dazzled by the sun. The second protest was even feebler than the first. 'Luke...'

He sucked more strongly, his teeth grating against her skin, creating tiny needles of pain that were instantly soothed by the moist movements of his mouth. And she lay there and submitted, watching him watching her over the top of her toes. His gaze was intense with a dark concentration. She had never thought of her feet as erogenous zones before, but the delicious sensation of bone-melting pleasure she was experiencing made her re-evaluate her thinking. No wonder people developed foot fetishes!

Suddenly she felt his tongue join the suckling, swirling and rasping against her wet skin. One of his hands slid lightly down the top of her foot and around behind her ankle, to drift up the back of her supple calf, his spreading fingers offering caressing support to the tautly extended muscle. The long, slow French kissing continued until Rosalind squirmed, a brief groan escaping her lips.

He lifted his mouth fractionally. 'Am I hurting you? Do you want me to stop?' His lips brushed against her sole as they formed the gruff words and she gave another little shivery moan. He was kneeling like a supplicant yet his eyes seemed to smoulder with the triumphant recognition of his own power. He knew *exactly* what he was doing to her...

Alarm bells started to ring in her distracted senses. The audacity of his action had been so out of character that it had caught her completely off guard, but she mustn't allow him to think that he could control and manipulate her through her passions.

'You're not hurting me...but I still think you'd better stop,' she asserted regretfully.

He lowered her foot onto his knee, holding her heel against the sun-warmed hardness of bone and muscle.

'I think whatever it was has come out anyway,' he said. His tongue appeared between his lips and he dabbed at it and then inspected his fingertip. 'Ah, yes, I'm sure it did...'

Rosalind suddenly remembered that her injury had supposedly been imaginary. 'Can I see?' She propped herself up on her hands but even as she spoke he was casually flicking whatever was on his fingertip into the breeze.

'Sorry, but it was hardly worth looking at. Such a tiny thing to cause you so much discomfort,' he said, so blandly that Rosalind's suspicions were reawakened.

But no, that was silly! Luke would never have summoned the nerve to make such an outrageously seductive move on purpose.

Would he?

'What made you want to try to get it out like that anyway?' she asked, thinking that tax avoidance was actually a fairly devious field requiring a certain amount of risk-taking by its practitioners. And Luke was a self-declared specialist.

'I saw it once...in a Bond movie,' he admitted.

Rosalind recalled the scene...and the way the woman's gratitude had been expressed afterwards, in typical Bond-girl fashion. She delivered him a tart warning. 'You should know that things you see done in the movies don't always work out the same in real life!'

'No, only sometimes,' he agreed meekly, his gaze briefly brushing her treacherously firm breasts. Rosalind shifted her foot hastily back onto the sand and as she did so the slight bristliness of his leg struck a familiar chord.

Her green eyes narrowed, squinting for a better look as she blurted out, 'For goodness' sake, Luke, do you *shave* your *legs*?'

'As a matter of fact, I do,' he said coolly, moving around beside her. 'I cycle, and shaving your legs makes treating the scrapes much less painful if you fall on the tarmac, not to mention reducing drag and chafing of the Lycra kit...'

'Oh.' Rosalind had discovered something else equally intriguing. 'You shave your chest too, don't you?'

She couldn't resist reaching over and touching it. His skin was like hot satin, slipping against her fingers, smooth but with a faint catch in a broad area from collar- to breast-bone. She guessed that in his natural state he would be quite furry.

His voice also had a slight, uneven catch. 'We wear Lycra body-shirts as well.'

Rosalind drew back, her fingers drifting absently to her parted lips, and the clean, salty tang of him suddenly filled her nostrils, creating an unexpected hunger. Her tongue crept out to touch her fingertips and now the taste of him was inside her too, lush and tempting...

Through a veil of lashes she watched Luke's eyes glaze at her action and then sink down her half-reclining body, drifting into intimate territory before faltering and returning to find the flaw in the otherwise pearly perfection of her skin.

His lips parted, his brows darting upwards in a slight frown. He bent over to trace the faint silvery line low down on her abdomen with his finger.

'What's this? Appendix?'

It was like being delicately brushed with a live wire. Rosalind's skin quivered and she could feel the downy-fine hair on her belly spring erect. His finger jerked away, only to return almost immediately to explore the tiny ridge. He was getting bolder by the minute.

'No!'

She had thought she had herself under control but suddenly she was fighting a fierce, almost overwhelming urge to plunge her fingers into the fine, silky hair that had slid across his temples, twine them amongst the sun-warmed strands and force his mouth slowly, slowly down to her body...to feel him move his open lips against that small, inoffensive, earth-shattering scar. And then, and then...

She put a flat hand just below his shoulder, hesitating when she felt his heart pumping as violently as hers, then she pushed him away—a hard shove that sent him sprawling on the sand.

He blinked up at her. 'What's the matter?'

'Nothing. I just think it's time we made a move!' she said, leaping up, her jerky movements revealing her inner agitation.

'I'm sorry; I didn't mean to dredge up bad memories for you,' he said, rolling lithely to his feet beside her, brushing the sand off his side.

'You didn't. It's just an operation scar—from years ago...when I was living in London.'

She could probably tell him the exact day if she wanted to dwell on it. But she had long ago decided that she wouldn't because that would mean dwelling on Justin— wonderful, laughing, handsome Justin—the first and last great love of her life, the shining knight of her dreams who had turned out to be utterly without honour or conscience.

Rosalind—young, passionately in love and blinded by her own romantic idealism—had been a willing victim of his forceful charm. Because her trust had been as absolute as her love she had ignored the most elementary precautions with the man she had expected to marry, only to find out that he had been unfaithful with a string of one-night stands.

She had been lucky. She could have faced a death sentence for her naïvety. As it was, the consequences of her liaison with Justin had sent her recklessly off the rails for a while, but she had quickly realised the self-destructive futility of her actions. Yes, something precious had been taken away from her, but she had since found other things, other blessings to put in its place...

'Were you involved in an accident?'

'No. Pelvic inflammatory disease.'

Her bluntness didn't embarrass him into silence. He frowned. 'It must have been serious for them to operate.'

'It was. And no, before you ask, I didn't get it by being promiscuous,' she bit out. Many people associated PID with sexual profligacy, but until Justin had charmed his way into her heart Rosalind had been remarkably chaste. Ironically her innocence had probably been her downfall. If she *had* been more sexually experienced she might have been less submissive to Justin's seductive wiles.

'What made it so serious?'

'There were complications...'

'What kind of complications?'

She looked at him incredulously. He seemed utterly in earnest. For a shy man he was showing a hell of a nerve! She began to laugh. 'Do you just want the highlights or should I get my doctor to send you a complete gynaecological history?'

He flushed, reverting to type, and she was reassured sufficiently to tease, 'Don't worry Luke, the only thing you've risked with me so far is foot-and-mouth disease.'

His flush deepened and she took advantage of his confusion to tell him that, since he had suddenly turned out to be such a hotshot windsurfer, *he* could sail the board back, while she strolled leisurely back to the hotel for some much needed R and R.

The School for Flirts was out for the day!

# CHAPTER SEVEN

FROM her vantage point beside a pillar in the glass wall Rosalind watched the man in shorts and singlet sweating on one of the ferocious torture machines inside the air-conditioned hotel gym.

'Crazy guy, huh?'

She jumped as someone came up beside her—a bouncy young Australian woman who had been taking an early-morning dip in the pool when Rosalind had passed it on her way to the reception desk to pick up some more of her money from her safety-deposit box.

'He looks in pain,' said Rosalind, wincing as Luke moved over to a free-weight bench-press and began another set of punishing exercises.

'Nah, I don't think those guys know what pain is— push a button and they just keep going and going. Most of them look as if you could knock them over with a feather... but their strength is in their incredible stamina—'

'What guys?' interrupted Rosalind, bewildered.

'Triathletes.'

'Did *he* tell you he was a triathlete?' she asked, hiding her amusement. If Luke had been practising some creative self-aggrandisement she didn't want to ruin it for him by blowing his cover.

'No, but I was in Hawaii last year when my father was doing PR work for one of the sponsors of the Ironman... I remember him—' she jerked her bleached-blonde head towards the gym '—because he was staying at the same hotel, scarfing up mountains of pasta and cake at the carbo-loading the day before the race. I actually saw him finish, too, quite well up in the field...'

Her words took a few moments to sink in properly. 'Luke was in the *Ironman*?' Rosalind repeated feebly.

*Her* Luke? The man she had privately voted the most likely to have sand kicked in his face... taking part in the most gruelling athletic event in the world?

Rosalind stormed through the glass doors into the gym and marched across to loom over Luke's supine figure on the padded bench-press.

'So this is why we have to have a late breakfast—so you can hang out with the rest of the jocks!' she flung at him accusingly, ignoring the fact that except for Luke the gym was deserted.

His hands almost slipped on the bar he was holding at the full extension of his arms. 'Roz! What are you doing here?' He lowered the weights on straining arms until the bar rested across his chest, his expression glazing protectively as he took in her glittering fury. 'Uh, you know the only reason I suggested breakfasting a bit later was to give you time to get over your nausea—'

'Oh, really?' She produced an exquisite sneer, unappeased. 'Not because you wanted to sneak out and pump some *iron* on the sly?'

His hair had flopped sweatily over his eyebrows and Rosalind was infuriated by a strong urge to comb it back. Even lying there clutching a set of massive weights, he still managed to project an air of defencelessness. 'Well, no, I—'

'Not because you're feeling deprived of your daily dose of self-flagellation?' she said, reminding herself that he was a hardened athlete. Physically, he was about as defenceless as a tank!

'Huh?'

'You know... those things you mild-mannered tax accountants do for a bit of relaxation...swimming, cycling, running? Hawaii Ironman?' she crunched out. 'Am I ringing any bells here yet, Mr Aw-gee-shucks-I'm-so-helpless James?'

Luke's chest contracted under his sweat-soaked singlet, his arms cording as he lifted the weight back onto the rack above him with only a faint grunt of effort. He sat up and swung his legs off the bench, using the small towel around his neck to blot his damp face and throat. 'That was your opinion. I never claimed to be helpless.'

Rosalind slapped her hands onto the hips of her ribbed cotton shorts. 'Oh, right,' she agreed with acid disbelief. 'And I suppose you'd never windsurfed before yesterday either!'

He had the grace to look guilty. 'Only once or twice, although I did quite a bit of board-surfing when I was young. We lived near a beach and I was a member of the local surf club. That's where I first got interested in triathlons...'

An ex-surfie! Rosalind ground her teeth, thinking of all the time she had spent trying to get him to balance upright on the board.

'I suppose in triathletes' parlance "once or twice" means you did a return crossing of the Pacific!' she said, sarcasm dripping from every word as her suspicions were confirmed. 'So you *were* deliberately having me on yesterday.'

'Well, maybe just a little,' he admitted, carrying out a few discreet warm-down stretches against the bench as she stood glowering at him, her lemon-yellow shorts and vest-top shimmering with her heaving outrage. When Rosalind's temper was sparking she didn't hold anything back.

'Fair's fair, Rosalind—you've been having plenty of fun at *my* expense ever since we met,' he pointed out. 'And you never *asked* me if I played any sport. I told you I had a full life but all you seemed interested in was my lack of cultural and social pursuits.'

She hated it when he used logic to make her feel in the wrong. 'Triathletes don't *play* at what they do,' she countered. 'I've read all about it. It's not a sport, it's an obsession.'

'Not for me. I just do it as a hobby—for fun.'

'Fun?' She stared at him, her anger eclipsed by her horror. If his idea of fun was to try to push himself beyond the limits of human endurance then he was even more socially deprived than she had thought! Maybe this new perspective of him wasn't so different from the old one. How typical of Luke to choose a solo sport. The tightness inside her loosened further as she contemplated all the solitary hours he must spend in training. No wonder he didn't have time for any other activities.

'You needn't look as though I've admitted to some gross depravity.' His eyebrows quirked in amusement. 'You ought to try it some time, Roz—the running part, I mean. There's no drug that can match the natural high it gives you.'

She smothered an unwilling grin. 'Since I don't do drugs I wouldn't know,' she said, exploding another colourful media myth. 'As a matter of fact I have my own version of a natural high...I get it from performing in front of a live audience.'

'You must be suffering a few withdrawal symptoms by now, then,' he said, with more accuracy than he could know. He glanced down at the trendy white designer sports shoes she was wearing. 'Look, since you've cut short my programme, why don't you come on a little run with me now, along the track at the back of the beach?'

'Ha! What do I look like—a masochist? You'd run me into the ground!'

'I'll go at your pace,' he offered. 'Come on; if your connection with your twin is putting your body under stress you could probably do with a little extra conditioning.'

She snapped at the challenge. 'I'm in perfect shape for my lifestyle, thank you very much!'

It was meant as a haughty rejection, so how was it that half an hour later she was bending over against the drunken U-shape of a wind-distorted palm tree at the side of the trail, desperately trying to suck another breath into her shattered lungs?

'Do you think you're going to be sick?' The fact that Luke's words were crisp and even, without the slightest hint of a puff, added insult to injury as far as Rosalind was concerned.

'This isn't morning sickness, it's exhaustion!' came tearing out of her throat between whistling breaths. 'I *told* you you'd run me into the ground.'

'But I was pacing myself to your stride—'

'Yes, well...I was showing off, wasn't I?' she wheezed, giving up on her dignity.

'Can't you catch your breath? Here, try this way.' Luke stood behind her and looped his arms under hers, lifting them straight up over her head so that she was forced into an upright, shoulders-back stance. 'Now try slow and deep rather than fast and shallow.'

Immediately the tightness in her chest eased and she found that her breathing slowed enough for her to joke, 'I guess that's me off the team, huh?'

'I should have realised you were pushing it, but you acted OK with the pace right up until you stopped.' His voice was rough with self-accusation.

'You've only now figured out what a great actress I am?' She tipped her bright head back against his shoulder, feeling the smooth power of his raised bicep brush her cheek. She could feel the heat and dampness of his chest through her thin top. His heart, she was chagrined to register, was barely skipping a beat, while hers was still going crazy.

'Do you ever switch off or are you always on, always acting a part for the person you're with?'

She stiffened at the unexpected thrust and tried to pull her arms down. '*You* can talk.'

His breath was hot on her nape as he steadied her in position. 'Not yet; just wait until your heartbeat slows a little more. Trust me—you'll feel better in a minute.'

She realised that his fingers around her wrists could feel her pounding pulse. Trapped by her fresh awareness of his superior strength and fitness, she resorted to striking back with words.

'*Trust* you? Why should I trust someone who pretends to be something he's not...who can't even be open with me about something as innocent as what he does in his spare time?'

His fingers tightened briefly. 'I'm Luke James. I've never pretended to be anyone else. Unlike *you*—'

'I had good reasons.'

'Escaping publicity? Oh, come on; publicity is something you've always thrived on.' He suddenly let her wrists go, his loosely encircling hands sliding the length of her arms as she lowered them to her sides and felt her fingers tingle with the returning blood.

He gripped her shoulders and spun her around to face him. She was shocked by his darkly intense expression and the rigid tension that gripped his entire body. She realised that she had finally goaded him into real anger. There was no gentle diffidence in him now, no shy uncertainty. The adrenalin which had been pumping into his system during the run was still saturating his blood.

'No, there's much more to it than avoiding a few newspaper reporters, isn't there, Rosalind?' he said harshly. 'I'm an intelligent man. Do you think I haven't realised why you practically dragooned me into letting you take over my holiday? It isn't solely for my benefit, is it? All I am to you is a distraction to keep your mind off whatever it is you're running away from...'

'That's not true—'

'Isn't it? *Isn't it?*'

'No!' Her gaze faltered, even though she realised at
that moment that it was indeed the literal truth. That
*wasn't* all he was to her, not by a long chalk...

She stepped back, and found her buttocks coming hard
up against the dipping curve of the misshapen palm that
she had grabbed to catch her breath. She clutched at it
again as Luke simultaneously mirrored her movement,
leaning forward to brace his hands on either side of her
hips, trapping her even more effectively than he had a
few moments before, this time in a position in which he
could read every nuance of her expression.

'Your personality shines with such incandescent
brightness that most people are too dazzled to see the
shadows,' he said quietly. 'What are they, Roz? What
is it that makes you run?'

'Apart from you, you mean?' She couldn't look away
from the hypnotic black gaze. She had an odd sensation
of falling and the even odder one of knowing that she
could rely on Luke to catch her, that he would be a
steady, rock-solid support. Perhaps he did have the right
to some answers, she thought, and by giving them to
him perhaps she might find out something she needed
to know.

So she told him about the bombardment of letters and
gifts she had been receiving from an unknown fan, about
her efforts to ignore the growing sense of menace in his
attentions. This time she made no attempt to make her
experience sound amusing and, lured on by Luke's silence
she found herself impulsively exposing the heart of her
anxiety—the stage fright that had caused her to question
the core of her belief in herself.

'All my life all I've ever wanted to be is an actress,'
she said starkly. 'It's what I've worked for. It's what I
*am.*'

'You mean it's the only thing in your life that you take
seriously.' Luke broke his silence with a sudden, shrewd
insight into the essence of her bright, bubbly, fun-loving

character. He felt a savage rush of pure adrenalin as he fitted a major piece into the elusive puzzle that was Roz Marlow. No wonder she had so few inhibitions about enjoying the pleasures of life—because she knew how truly inessential such things were to her happiness. The social butterfly flitted compulsively not because she was unable to care deeply enough about anyone or anything to commit but because she was already committed elsewhere.

'If I can't perform, if I'm not Rosalind Marlow the actress, who am I? My parents offered me this holiday as a kind of escape, but I suppose the one thing that I'm never going to escape is myself...'

'And you have absolutely no idea who this Peter is...?'

She almost—*almost*—said a name.

The relief would have been enormous.

But she couldn't permit herself the luxury. If Rosalind mentioned Peter Noble by name, Luke would want to know why she hadn't reported him to the police. He would want to know who he was and how Rosalind had found out about him.

How could she tell him that Peter was Peggy Staines's illegitimate son, given up for adoption after a secret teenage pregnancy? Peggy had been adamant that no one else was to know. She had never even told her husband about the bitter mistake that haunted her past and she had been appalled when her adult son had somehow traced her and confronted her one day when she was out shopping.

For weeks she had been torn between curiosity about the baby she had been forced to give up all those years ago and fear of the moody adult that he had become. She'd been especially afraid that Peter's persistent attempts to make her accept him in her life would result in the old shame becoming public and thus jeopardise her marriage and her husband's all-important career. To add to her guilt, she had found out that Peter had not been happy with his adoptive family, which had broken up and dispersed when he was a teenager.

In an attempt to placate both Peter and her conscience, Peggy had agreed to visit him at his flat, but the more she'd seen of him, the more disturbed she had become by his erratic behaviour. She'd discovered that he had been an outpatient at a psychiatric clinic and her fears about his mental stability had seemed to be confirmed after she'd seen his bizarrely decorated flat and realised the extent to which his fan-worship of his favourite actress had taken over his life.

Peter had no job and was on limited medical benefit, yet in his closet he'd had a complete wardrobe of expensive new clothes in Rosalind's size, still with their sales tags attached, and a range of her favourite make-up and toiletries lined up beside his razor in the bathroom. A home-made pin-up calendar of Rosalind had been marked with a detailed log of her activities, and when Peggy had found copies of his letters to Rosalind she had panicked at the thought of what would happen if Peter got into trouble and was exposed to the public spotlight.

Rosalind's knowledge from here on was very sketchy, because by the time she had met Peggy in that infamous hotel room the distraught woman had worked herself into such a state that she had only had time to sob out the bare bones of her story before she had succumbed to the pain of her heart attack, gasping incoherently about something that Peter had done that had made all her soul-searching and suffering pointless...

Rosalind, who had just got out of the shower and had still been in her damp robe when her visitor had arrived at her hotel room fully two hours early for their meeting, hadn't been quite quick enough when Peggy had suddenly crumpled to the floor. In spite of the choking pain, she had struggled vainly to communicate, only subsiding when a frightened Rosalind had firmly promised that she wouldn't do or say anything to anyone about Peter until she had Peggy's permission.

Now she was trapped by the integrity that the Press claimed she didn't possess. It was ironic that in order to produce proof of her honour she would have to violate it.

'I know that it's someone who's much more disturbed than I wanted to believe,' she sighed, hoping that Luke hadn't read the long pause as significant.

'Then why haven't you *done* something about it?' he demanded, his impatience reeking of disapproval.

'I guess I felt—feel—sort of sorry for the guy,' she admitted, the mingled scents of cologne and male sweat rising between their bodies making her aware of how close they were standing. With Luke leaning in on her, his arms splayed around her sides, anyone coming up the trail behind them would think that they were embracing...

'*Sorry* for him?' Luke's exasperation with her tolerance was almost identical to Jordan's and expressed equally forcefully. 'He doesn't need your sympathy, Roz; what he *needs* is to be stopped before he can harm you or himself.'

Rosalind shivered in the steamy morning heat. 'I know.' She pulled a face. 'Jordan suggested I acquire a bodyguard for the duration.'

He frowned. 'Which you refused, of course.'

He was much better at predicting her behaviour than she was at guessing his reactions. She gave a defensive shrug.

'I already have too many people following me everywhere. If a crazed fan did try an abduction the reporters would descend like a cloud of locusts. They'd soon scare him off!'

'And ruin the chance to spin out a good story? More likely they'd stand back and take pictures,' he said grimly. 'You're lucky you've got the Staines affair hanging over your head, or you wouldn't even have the minimal protection of press surveillance.'

Her eyes flashed at the unexpected callousness of the remark. 'There's nothing lucky about it! Mrs Staines is still seriously ill in hospital, you know.'

'*Mrs Staines?*' he repeated, his eyebrows flicking derisively upwards. 'Isn't that a rather formal way to refer to someone you've been having secret assignations with— surely you're on first-name terms with each other?'

The sting in his tone hit her on the raw. 'It was only *one* assignation, damn it!' she blurted out. 'It was the first time we'd ever met!'

His seething impatience seemed to still, his voice easing to a toneless neutrality. 'That must have made it all the more traumatic for you when she collapsed like that.'

Rosalind lowered her head, biting her bottom lip as she replayed her own actions in her mind. 'I suppose I can't help feeling as if it was my fault, even though the whole thing was her idea...' She was so intent on the disturbing memory that she didn't notice Luke stiffen slightly. 'I've never seen anyone have a heart attack before. There was so little I could do. It was *dreadful*. I hated being so helpless...'

'I know the feeling.'

His quiet anger jolted Rosalind out of her self-absorption.

'Do you?' She lifted her face to his and saw a bleakness in his brooding countenance that pierced her to the heart. Without thinking she reached up and laid a comforting hand against his rigid cheek. He froze, and his eyes searched hers, then dropped to her pink mouth, which was slightly swollen from her thoughtful nibbling, and she was suddenly breathless all over again, taking shallow sips of air that gave her no respite from the tightness in her chest.

'Luke...?'

'What?' His voice was thick, his cheek heavy in her hand as he leaned his head into her touch, rubbing at her like a giant cat being petted, the corner of his mouth brushing the sensitive mound at the base of her thumb as he spoke.

'I think...'

'What?' He turned his head completely, his mouth opening against the centre of her palm, his eyes flaring darkly at the taste of her, the cold bleakness in their depths disappearing, leaving a smouldering awareness in its wake. He moved abruptly closer, bringing his hips firmly against hers, pushing her backwards against the trunk of the palm, his arms closing in until they brushed her sides.

'What do you think, Rosalind...?'

His hoarse, muffled whisper made her head spin. Whatever it was no longer seemed important. The important thing was that Luke's breath was moist and hot in her cupped hand and his bent knee was softly insinuating itself between hers, pressing forward and then retreating until, unable to bear the sensual torment any more, she widened her stance, eagerly inviting the added intimacy. He came the rest of the way in a rush, roughly pushing into the space she had created for him and drawing his other leg sharply against her flank, compressing her thigh between warm pillars of taut muscle.

For some perverse reason she kept her hand over his mouth while the centres of their bodies kissed, shifted and kissed again, her other hand applying pressure to his chest, preventing his torso from crushing against her breasts. She was excited by the stormy look in Luke's eyes as he submitted reluctantly to the delicate restraint. She was playing power games with him and they both knew it. They knew that he was stronger and fitter and could easily overcome her token resistance if he chose. But he didn't choose, because he was too much of a gentleman, and maybe because he was a little in awe of her feminine power, thought Rosalind exultantly.

That didn't mean, however, that he didn't possess other means of persuasion. Denied the luxury of taste, he resorted to his other most potent sense to appease their mutual craving for contact, holding her gaze as he rocked against her, grinding her soft buttocks into the rough palm-trunk, his muscles quivering with strain. He was wild for more, and so was Rosalind, but she wanted to tease, to withhold the pleasure that she knew was awaiting them for another few, dizzyingly delicious moments.

He made a deep, smothered sound in his chest and she felt his stiffened tongue dart into a crease between her clamped fingers—a blunt, wet probe that she resisted, even as it made her go weak at the knees. His eyes were sullen, raging with a strange mixture of anger and desire, and hints of a sultry male challenge that thrilled her to her toes. This was Luke the athlete, superbly self-disciplined and intensely focused on his own state of physical readiness. Her mouth went dry, a swimmy heat hazing everything but the man sharply centred in her vision.

Rosalind licked her lips, unconsciously tempting him with what she had denied him. His tongue thrust again at her fingers and she felt his thighs simultaneously tense around her trapped leg, squeezing and releasing in a graphic rhythm that made her arch her hips in the instinctive feminine response.

His control slipped a notch and his hands released their white-knuckled grip on the tree-trunk beside her hips and contracted around her waist, his fingers sizzling on her skin where her vest-top had ridden up from the waistband of her shorts. He angled his body, bending Rosalind further back over the curving beam of the palm, until the tendons in her neck ached with the effort of keeping him in sight and every cell and nerve-end between her knees and her waist was imprinted with the indelible evidence of his masculinity.

'All right!' she gasped, whipping her hand from his mouth.

'All right what?' he growled savagely.

She slid her arms around his taut neck, her fingers linking tightly across his strong nape, supporting herself while at the same time attempting to pull him down. 'All right, you can kiss me,' she ordered flatly, and was shocked to find him suddenly resisting. 'What's the matter?' she husked, rotating the bony jut of her hip against the hard resilience between his spread thighs. 'Changed your mind?'

'Lost it, more like,' was the ragged answer, half under his breath. His head dipped closer at her urging. 'Why am I letting you do this to me?'

Her eyes glowed with cat-like satisfaction at his whisper of helpless fascination. He was admitting that he was hers, to do with as she pleased ...

'Don't tell me I have to teach you how to kiss as well as how to flirt?' she murmured invitingly.

He was breathing harshly, his black eyes riveted on her pouting mouth as he struggled with his self-control. 'What's to teach? A kiss is just a kiss ...'

She laughed—a sound of pure feminine provocation. 'Oh, Luke, do you have a *lot* to learn ...'

Her condescending mockery was smothered by his urgent mouth. It was hot and hard and surprisingly tart. His lips slanted across hers, his tongue smoothing inside the velvety interior of her mouth, sucking at the sweetness he found there.

Rosalind's eyes fluttered shut, unable to cope with the sensual overload. She was in a dark world of heat and tumultuous sensation which intensified when she felt his hands drifting up and down her satiny sides under the thin vest-top, his thumbs shaping the tender outer swell of her breasts exposed by her skimpy bra.

His teeth grazed her lips, his hardness lodged tightly in the hollow of her groin, and his fingertips slid under her lacy straps on their next casual journey, curling around the narrow ribbons and peeling the stretchy fabric down, leaving her breasts peaking against the soft abrasion of her top.

Rosalind's hands slid up into his hair, gripping him hard and deepening the kiss as she waited in exquisite agony for the explorative touch to steal back up to the flesh he had daringly exposed, but his hands stayed inexplicably at her waist, fingers kneading the soft indentation with an almost painful thoroughness. She twisted restlessly. She couldn't bear him to turn tentative and shy on her, not *now* ... She clutched at his wrists, dragging his hands up under her top and moulding them around her naked breasts.

Fireworks went off in her head. A convulsion of indescribable pleasure rolled over her, enveloping every millimetre of her skin from the top of her tingling scalp to the tips of her reflexively curled-up toes. The heated darkness came rushing up at her like a physical force, sweeping away any semblance of thought or will, sucking her into a black hole of pure, concentrated sensation. Time warped and stretched, turning fluid and meaningless. The universe shrank at an accelerating rate until it was composed of nothing but a warm body and a violently beating heart...one man at the centre of eternity.

It was Luke who broke the blindingly erotic spell, Luke who dragged his mouth away from hers, his hands still moving compulsively on her breasts, violent tremors shaking his body as he fought the gravitational pull of their mutual desire.

'God, what am I doing?' he muttered harshly, dragging his hands from her bare flesh but unable to prevent his fingers trailing a final, reluctant farewell across her stiffened nipples as he did so, his eyes burning at the sight of her instinctive little shudder of response.

Rosalind stared up at him in dazed confusion until the tortured self-contempt in his expression brought reality crashing back down on her. She too was trembling, only the palm tree behind her hips preventing her from sinking bonelessly to her knees in front of the man who had kidnapped her senses and held them so ravishingly to ransom.

She hadn't wanted to be rescued, she realised helplessly. She hadn't cared what they were doing, or where, or why. One minute she had been a playful temptress confident of her control, the next she had been a maelstrom of chaotic emotions, utterly at the mercy of her feelings for this one man. Luke James.

His thin mouth twisted at her wide-eyed stare, mistaking it for challenge. 'Well, teacher, I guess you made your point,' he said, stepping back.

'Did I?' It was Rosalind who had learned a lesson, and she was still grappling with the terrifying implications.

'I'm sorry if I hurt you.'

'What?' She had pulled her bra back over her breasts and now her hands flattened defensively over their aching tenderness, protecting her lingering arousal from his mockery.

To her shock he touched her throbbing mouth with his thumb, his face grave. 'I didn't realise I was being so rough... you have a little cut...'

'It doesn't hurt,' she said hastily, turning aside, so that his touch slid to the outer point of her jaw, a brief streak of fire across her soft cheek.

He straightened, putting his hands behind his back, and Rosalind didn't doubt that his fists were clenched as he said tightly, 'I suppose I should thank all your previous lovers for providing my teacher with her expertise.'

*Previous* lovers? That implied that she had a current one. A jealous lover who had the right to delve into all the secrets of her soul, who would seduce her from her emotional independence with the promise of something infinitely more rewarding, something she yearned for beyond the expression of words. Panic rose in Rosalind's throat and she resorted to her protective cloak of flippancy.

'Oh, not *all* of them,' she drawled. 'Out of the legion of men I've had in my bed there were one or two who were totally uninspiring.'

'Has there really been a legion?' he asked, his eyes narrowing at the defiant glitter in hers.

'At least!'

'Do you know how much a legion is, according to the dictionary definition?'

She shrugged airily. 'A lot.'

'Three to six thousand.'

Rosalind's jaw dropped and so did Luke's eyelids.

'That's an awful lot of lovers for any one woman,' he said smoothly.

'Well, maybe that's a little on the high side,' she said weakly.

'Only a little?' His eyebrow etched the daring question. It wasn't often that he had Rosalind so thoroughly off balance and he intended to press his advantage.

'Shall we just say I'm considerably less experienced than most people seem to think?' she said, wryly conceding him his victory.

He showed an unfortunate tendency to rub it in. 'How much less?'

'I don't think that's any of your business, do you?' she retorted, ruffled by his persistence. She wondered what Luke would say if she told him that the reason why she was such an expert in light-hearted flirtation was that she had been celibate for years. Turning aside propositions without wounding egos or losing valued friendships took a practised sleight of tongue.

'After what nearly happened just now I think it is,' he said with a quiet, unnerving certainty that prompted an instant, knee-jerk objection.

'Nothing *happened*—'

'I said *nearly*,' he corrected her, his eyes dropping to where her nipples still thrust against her thin top. 'But I don't happen to think that what we did was "nothing". It certainly felt like something to me. I'm afraid I don't have your sophistication—I don't quite know how to handle this…attraction between us…I don't know what to do.'

For a shattering moment she took him literally. 'You don't mean that you've never—? That you're a…a…?' She stepped away from the mind-blowing thought and trod on a cylindrical piece of coral on the uneven track. Her ankle twisted as her foot skated away, sending her down on one knee amongst the crushed shells.

'Steady!' He picked her up and set her on her slender legs again, bending to brush at the shell-dust that mingled with the blood that seeped from the minor scrape. 'You don't have to propose to get me into your bed,' he said, straight-faced. 'I didn't mean I was *that* innocent. Is your ankle all right?'

'It's fine,' she said dismissively, ignoring the slight stinging of her grazed flesh as she watched him straighten and reveal his lightly flushed face. 'Then what *did* you mean? How many lovers have there been in *your* murky past?'

He hesitated before answering briefly. 'One.'

Rosalind felt instantly light-headed. 'One what? One important one? One legion?'

He didn't smile. 'One lover. My wife.'

'You're *married*?' she whispered, her honey-coloured complexion paling, making her incredulous green eyes look enormous. She was profoundly shocked, even more so than when she had gone to a party she had thought she would have to miss and surprised Justin in the act of infidelity with one of his nameless pick-ups. At least with Justin she had been prepared by her growing suspicions. And somehow Luke seemed to be the type to wear a wedding ring...strait-laced, strictly honourable...

'I was. She died.'

Rosalind was appalled by her sense of relief and rushed to atone for her inappropriate emotions. 'I'm sorry.'

'It was a long time ago.' He put a hand under her elbow, turning her in the direction of the hotel. 'Come on, we'll walk the rest of the way back. I've got some antibiotic cream I can use to clean up that cut.'

'If it was a long time ago you must have married very young...' Curiosity crawled through Rosalind's veins as she limped gracefully along beside him. What had his wife been like? she wondered.

Was she pretty? she asked him silently. Did she make you laugh? Did she make you happy? If she was alive would you still love her?

'I was nineteen and Christie was eighteen.'

She turned that over in her mind. He would still have been at university. Hadn't he said he had lived with his parents?

'Did you *have* to get married?'

As soon as the question left her lips Rosalind's curiosity faltered. What if Christie had had a baby? Children? Luke could be a father, for all she knew. A family man. Someone who loved children and believed that procreation was the essential purpose of marriage.

'Quite the reverse,' he said firmly. 'Christie and I were sweethearts all through our teens but she came from a very religious family, even stricter than mine. There was no question of sex before marriage.'

'Oh.'

He intercepted her sideways glance and judged it correctly. 'And yes, that *is* one of the reasons we got married so young,' he admitted drily. 'We were both mature for our age and very sure of our feelings, and our parents realised that we were having more and more difficulty in refraining from the full expression of our love. They were happy to approve a marriage that would avert a sin.'

The chalets were in sight and Rosalind shortened her steps to a dawdle, forcing Luke to do the same as she tried to keep him talking. 'So how long were you married?'

'A year.' The casualness with which he spoke belied the horror of what he was saying as he added matter-of-factly, 'Although we only spent five days actually living together as husband and wife. Christie was critically injured in a car accident on the way back from our honeymoon. A man had a heart attack at the wheel and slammed into us from a side-road. Christie never regained consciousness.'

Rosalind felt some vital yet nameless defence crumble inside her, his words issuing from a well of loneliness that echoed in the empty chambers of her heart. 'Oh, Luke, no...'

They had reached his door, but he made no attempt to use the fact as an excuse to bring the conversation to a polite conclusion. He used his key and ushered Rosalind inside, then continued in that mildly detached voice, as if the tragic story related to an acquaintance rather than himself.

'What we had was so brief, yet so special... Christie and I always seemed to be utterly attuned to each other—heart, mind and soul. I knew I wouldn't find that kind of perfection with anyone else, so I never bothered to try. I just wasn't interested in platonic female companionship or empty physical release. Neither seemed to matter. If I ever looked at another woman in lust it was only because she reminded me in some way of Christie—'

'And me? Do _I_ remind you of Christie?' she interrupted as he sat her down on the bamboo couch and handed her a tissue from the hotel-branded box on the coffee-table. How could she be expected to worry about something as mundane as a minor scrape on her knee when he was performing open-heart surgery?

Her mouth went dry as she waited for him to tell her that, yes, Christie had been a slim, green-eyed redhead.

'There's no resemblance whatsoever.'

But as she started to breathe again his brutal scalpel of truth continued to flash. 'Yet I find myself wanting to have sex with you. I can't seem to stop myself thinking about it. Whenever I look at you, I imagine you—' He clenched his teeth and his hands at his sides, forcing the difficult words out. 'I think of how it would be with you ... I think of doing things with you that I—' A light sheen of sweat that had nothing to do with their run had broken out on his upper lip. 'And at night I have dreams—'

He broke off, but he didn't need to go on. Rosalind's hand trembled as she dabbed the tissue ineffectually against her knee, trying to look her most blasé when inside she was turning cartwheels like a giddy teenager. She had had a few fairly intense dreams herself...

'I see.'

He swept the hair impatiently off his forehead. 'I wish *I* did.' He looked angry, bewildered by his inability to explain his own behaviour, aggressive in his vulnerability.

Rosalind's defences dropped even further.

'Maybe it's *because* I'm so very different,' she offered gently. 'Maybe you've allowed yourself to feel desire for me because you know I'm not a threat to your memories of Christie.'

'But you are. I told you, Christie is the only woman I've ever made love to—'

'But it would be only sex with me, wouldn't it?' She proudly pointed out what he himself had made very clear. 'You can't *make love* with someone you don't love.'

'"Only sex",' he mimicked roughly. 'Is that all it is to you, Roz—"only" another incidental encounter with a person you fleetingly fancy?'

'As a matter of fact, no,' she said steadily, noting his careful use of language. 'I won't deny I did go through a brief period in my life when I wasn't very discriminating about *men*—' she hoped he noticed the special stress '—but I'd just been terribly hurt by someone whom I believed was the love of my life, and in typically flamboyant style I decided to show everyone how much I didn't care. I didn't want to be pitied. I thought that if I acted like Justin had it would somehow make *me* feel better. It didn't, so I stopped. I may flirt, but I don't sleep around.'

Her tilted chin and the thread of steely pride in her voice told him that he could take or leave it—she wasn't going to beg for his respect.

'I'll get that ointment for your knee,' he said quietly, and went up the stairs to his bathroom without further comment.

Rosalind brushed at the stupid blurring in her eyes and got up, thinking that a little flexing would stop her caked knee from hardening over and making it more difficult to treat. She walked over to the small dining table where Luke's computer lay open, plugged into the electrical outlet in the wall, a screen-saver busily at work. Maybe Luke had left it on because he was expecting a fax or some electronic mail, she thought.

The computer looked highly sophisticated, but appeared to have no mouse or trackball. Rosalind leaned over and ran her finger over the flat pad where she had expected the trackball to be. The screen-saver suddenly dissolved and she realised that the pad was a miniature touch-sensitive screen. She dragged her finger across it again and sure enough the little cursor arrow moved in a parallel course. She tapped and a file opened full-screen.

Guiltily, because she hadn't realised that the cursor was hovering over any particular icon, she dragged the arrow up to the 'close' box, and was about to tap when a name leapt out at her from the mass of single-spaced text.

Her own name...things that she had said...things that she had done.

Luke, it seemed, had been making detailed notes of their association from the day they had first met.

# CHAPTER EIGHT

'SPECTACULAR, isn't it?'

Rosalind didn't turn as the shadowy figure materialised on the ground beside her. Deep in the inky shadows of the casuarina tree, in her midnight-blue dress, she had thought she was invisible, but Luke evidently had eyes like a cat.

She kept her gaze fixed on the dark horizon. On Tioman the night was star-studded and clear but far out across the sea a distant electrical storm played out its fury. Sheet lightning flickered incessantly, brilliant flashes of varying intensity illuminating the rim of the world, throwing the billowing clouds high above the horizon into pulsating relief. There was no thunder, only the hushed breath of the sea to accompany the theatrical light-show, the violence of nature seeming all the more impressive for its silence.

When she didn't respond to his opening question she heard Luke shift on the soft carpet of dried casuarina needles scattered across the sandy soil.

'Where did you rush off to this morning? I looked for you. I thought we had plans...'

Rosalind could almost smell the ozone in the air, but it wasn't from the distant lightning. She felt electricity crackling through her veins, but, unlike the storm, her rage couldn't remain silent for long.

'I went on a parasailing trip. With the hunk from the pool bar,' she added with savage bite, not taking her eyes off nature's fireworks display.

There was a heartbeat's silence, then he said softly, and without a trace of jealousy, 'Trying to show me how much you don't care, in your typically flamboyant fashion, Roz?'

'Don't flatter yourself! It had nothing to do with you,' she lied desperately, appalled at how easily he'd turned her own words against her.

'Then why won't you talk to me?'

'Why? So you can make some more *notes*?' she spat, her skin crawling at the memory of scrolling through the screens of information about herself—her habits and likes and dislikes, what she'd worn and what she'd said—the conversations with Luke reported almost verbatim.

Until she'd seen it coldly written down she hadn't realised how much she'd unwittingly revealed during their harmless 'flirtation', not only about herself but about her family and friends, a number of whom were famous in their own right. She had *trusted* Luke at a time when her life was ripe with paranoia and this was how he'd repaid her!

Damn it, he was as bad as Justin... worse, because she knew now that what she had felt for Justin had been a romantic yearning that had ignored reality. She had been in love with the idea of being in love, with the notion of finding her perfect match, and Justin had seemed conveniently to fit the bill.

Luke was far from perfect and he had never tried to be her ideal. He was irritating and engaging, obstinate and agreeable, shy and bold, blunt and evasive... in short, a mass of contradictions that should have sent her screaming in the opposite direction. Instead she had been perversely fascinated, seduced by her growing appreciation of his complexity of character, his breadth of mind and the smouldering power of his subdued sexuality. Somewhere along the line, without even realising what was happening, Rosalind had started falling in love with him!

'Damn you, you've been *dissecting* me like some character in a *play*!' She blinked hard, grateful for the darkness and appalled at her pathetic desire to cry on the shoulder of the very man who had caused her pain.

His sharp counter-attack vanquished the momentary weakness. 'Oh, come on, Roz, you do exactly the same thing with everyone you meet. A gesture here, a character trait there... they're all grist to your actor's mill. As I *was going* to explain to you this morning, clarifying my thoughts about a person or a problem by writing them down is a habit of mine—my observations were purely for my own benefit. I have—*had*—no intention of showing my personal jottings to anyone else.'

His grim self-correction told her he now knew that she had not only wiped the file off his hard disk but had also stolen the back-up floppy which had been in the drive.

'For God's sake, Roz, surely you can't *still* think I'm an undercover journalist?'

She wished she did. At this point she would have been relieved to find out that he was simply an over-enthusiastic hack, because a far more disturbing alternative had arisen.

Luke's word-processing program had been person-alized with his full name. When Rosalind had inadver-tently opened her file the copyright box had appeared for several seconds, but only later in the day had the impact of it exploded on her consciousness like a bomb.

Luke Peter James.

One of his names was *Peter*.

It could be just a coincidence. It probably *was* just a coincidence, she had feverishly tried to convince herself.

He *couldn't* be Peter Noble. Peggy's son was unem-ployed and on benefit, and even if he had been tracking Rosalind's movements as precisely as Peggy had claimed he wouldn't have had access to the kind of information or money that would have enabled him to follow her to Tioman. Unless he included fraud amongst his obsessions...

But what if everything Peggy had told Rosalind about her son was wrong? After all, she only knew what Peter had chosen to tell her. Peggy had been far too afraid of stirring up the murky past to make any independent investigation into his background... she didn't even know if his story about his adoptive family was true. What if he had told Peggy a pack of lies? What if *Luke* was telling a pack of lies to Rosalind?

He himself had pointed out the dangers of making assumptions. Just because Rosalind had independent verification that he was a triathlete, that didn't mean that he couldn't also be a borderline psychotic. Maybe all that heartbreaking stuff about his wife dying was a scam to arouse her sympathy.

Of course, it was all absurdly unlikely, but the circumstantial evidence was very unnerving: Luke's name was also Peter, he was adopted and the same age that Peggy's son would be, he had torn out an article about Rosalind—perhaps to add to his extensive collection at home—and was keeping a detailed account of her every move.

If ridiculing the idea out of existence didn't work, she could just *ask* him—but if Luke *was* Peter Noble she might be safer pretending to be unaware. To acknowledge his obsession might be to validate it. Oh, *why* hadn't she spoken to the psychologist whom Jordan had urged her to consult about handling a personal confrontation with her psychotic fan? Because she had been too busy hoping it would never happen...

'Rosalind?' Luke persisted. Wasn't relentless persistence a sign of an obsessive mind? 'I said, you surely can't still believe I'm compiling a sleazy kiss-and-tell for some moronic magazine?'

At the reminder of the kisses they had shared an icy thrill of erotic fear coursed down her spine. Even now, wondering if Luke was her stalker, she felt the powerful tug of attraction, the insidious stirring of sexual curiosity.

Maybe *she* was the one who was deranged! Rosalind scrambled hastily to her feet, away from the temptation.

'There's nothing for you to tell anyway!' she said, hearing the amused contempt ring false in her own ears.

'Isn't there?' He rose more slowly, like a hunter wary of frightening his skittish prey. He seemed larger in the darkness and Rosalind's heart began to beat up into her throat.

'We kissed a few times, had a few laughs together— it didn't mean anything to either of us!' She quietly put one sandalled foot behind the other and began to shift her weight backwards.

'Didn't it?'

He was circling around her, and she turned to keep him within her night-blurred sight. She could hear her pulse in her ears, could feel but not see his eyes boring into her, and experienced the tingling of her scalp that usually presaged a severe attack of stage fright. Oh, God, if he *was* Peter she mustn't let him paralyse her in real life as she had let him do to her on stage.

'No!'

'Then why are you spitting at me like a cornered vixen? Could it be that you feel threatened by how much you enjoyed those *few laughs*...?'

It was such an apt description of her feelings that she recoiled. 'Damn you!'

His voice oozed with heavy satisfaction as he continued to pad softly around her, increasing his speed so that her head began to whirl as she tried to keep up with him, the hem of her halter-necked slip-dress flaring around her knees. 'No, damn *you* Roz. *You* started this game; we're not going to stop now, just because you've discovered that you don't get to make all the rules.'

She lifted her hands in a fierce warding-off gesture, some words from Shakespeare sliding unbidden into her mind. 'He was furnished like a hunter/O, ominous! he comes to kill my heart.'

'What game?' she said desperately. 'I don't know what you're talking about—'

His soft laugh was grim with determination.

'I'm talking about this...'

His mouth was as warm and exciting as she remembered, his body as hard, and once more her passionate nature was hostage to his fervent enthusiasm. She stopped struggling, her fear dissolving in the heat of a seductive yearning. What Luke lacked in finesse he certainly made up for in zeal. How could she be afraid of someone who made her feel so beautiful, so powerful, so desirable and, uniquely in her recent experience, so utterly *complete*?

Her trapped hands fluttered briefly against his lean flanks before her fingers curled into the rough linen weave of his softly gathered trousers, not tugging him closer, but not pushing him away either. Like her dress, Luke's shirt was made of silk, and the two whisper-thin surfaces were slippery against each other, generating a slick friction which, with every movement, every wild breath and ripple of muscle, made parts of Rosalind ache for a similar caress.

His mouth suddenly broke away and Luke leaned his forehead against hers, resting it there while his arms fell loosely to her hips, cradling them against his fierce arousal.

'You're right—however it started this isn't a game for us any more,' he panted raggedly. 'Let's stop teasing each other... to hell with all the rest. Come to bed with me, Roz... please... I won't hurt you, I'll protect you... Come back with me now and dazzle me with your splendour...'

The hunter was disarming himself before his captive prey.

'Come... dazzle me with your splendour...'

How could any woman resist such a poetic, impassioned plea?

Hours later Rosalind was still reliving the pleasure of that exquisite moment, and cursing the self-doubt which had smothered her impulse to accept his invitation. She had wanted to fling herself headlong into the reckless glory of loving Luke, but for the first time in her life her steadfast optimism had failed her. She had been afraid to trust her instincts, afraid that her judgement was warped by her feelings.

Rosalind Marlow, the wild child of tabloid journalism, afraid to take a risk. What a laugh!

Rosalind paced back and forth in her bedroom, her heart aching for the man she had deserted under the casuarina tree. Had he been hurt by the fierceness of her rejection? Maybe she had gone overboard in her attempt to sound as if she was still angry with him. Luke hadn't even tried to follow her... surely if he was obsessed with her he wouldn't have let her just walk away?

She stopped and pressed her ear against the wall. Still not a single sound or vibration from the next chalet. She rested her hot cheek against the cool paintwork and closed her eyes. Damn it, where *was* he? Why the hell wasn't he knocking at her door, pestering her to change her mind?

Because he wasn't Peter, that was why, her guilty conscience whispered. Luke was simply an honest man who had got out of his depth with a witchy woman who blew inexplicably hot and cold and acted mortally insulted when he paid her the supreme compliment of trying to understand her.

Where on earth could he have gone? To the bar, to drown his humiliation in vodka? Or... more likely from what she knew of Luke... had he gone for a long, solitary walk to brood over his sorrows?

Rosalind jerked upright. What if Luke fell victim to the dreaded ricochet effect? What if, in his wanderings, he encountered some shameless, man-eating hussy who offered him the opportunity to soothe his wounded male ego with some mindless sex? Her blood boiled with jealousy at the idea. She felt sick at the thought of him with any other woman.

Her green eyes narrowed grimly as she made up her mind. Luke had stopped short of making any emotional declarations but she sensed that he had strong feelings for her, otherwise he wouldn't be in such a turmoil.

This definitely wasn't just a physical attraction. If Rosalind loved him she couldn't keep running away from the responsibility, but nor could she blind herself to her suspicions, as she had done with Justin. The Justin she had thought she was in love with had been a flawless young god who had turned out to have feet of clay. Luke was a flesh-and-blood man who had attracted her *because* of his flaws, rather than in spite of them.

Still, this time she had much more to lose than her girlish dreams and Rosalind had to be certain with her heart *and* her head that she was doing the right thing for Luke as well as for herself. If she couldn't bring herself to take him on trust, well, she would have to take him without, and hope to make up for her lack of faith later...

First, and most important of all, she needed to reread what he had written about her—properly, from start to finish this time, instead of relying on the few jumbled extracts that had leapt at her from the screen that morning. She wanted to know just how much of his own feelings and motives he had recorded in his so-called 'diary'.

Grabbing the small computer disk from her bedside table, Rosalind went out onto the balcony and peered around the edge of the lattice screen at his darkened bedroom. She knew Luke would have locked the front door of his chalet when he'd gone out, but, as she had hoped, he had left his balcony sliding door slightly open.

For someone as nimble as Rosalind it was a matter of seconds to kick off her sandals and swing herself over the sturdy wooden rail. The computer disk between her teeth, she edged along the narrow wooden parapet until she was on the other side of the screen and clambered back over the rail.

The sliding door moved silently on its smooth track and Rosalind uttered a smothered giggle of nervous fright as the filmy white curtain suddenly billowed out of the widened gap to wrap itself around her. She fought her way free only to stub her toe on the raised track and stumble into the room with a whispered curse.

She would make a hopeless cat burglar, she thought, realising that she had dropped the precious disk and would have to waste time fumbling around on the floor in the darkness. She put out a hand and knocked it against the back of a cane chair. If only she could turn on a light...

The light clicked on beside the bed and she found herself staring at Luke, who was rumple-haired and crumple-eyed as he pushed himself upright, the sheet slithering down his bare chest to settle around his waist.

'Roz?'

'Luke!' she said faintly, shocked by the sight of him. He had been here all along! *Sleeping*, for God's sake, while she had been miserably pacing her chalet, agonising over his whereabouts! She put her hand up to her frantically beating heart, wondering how she was going to explain her presence in his bedroom.

It seemed that an explanation was not required. A beatific expression stole into his sleep-darkened eyes.

'Rosalind, you came!' He pushed back the bedclothes and rose to greet her, splendidly naked.

'I knew you would,' he said warmly, strolling towards her, his mouth curving in delighted welcome. 'I knew you'd change your mind and come to me...'

Not only naked, but also magnificently aroused and completely unselfconscious about it, thought Rosalind hazily as she watched his graceful stride eat up the distance between them. Poetry in motion...every muscle moving in well-oiled symmetry under his burnished skin, the smooth hairlessness of his chest, belly and legs accentuating the thick, dark brown cloud of curly hair at the juncture of his thighs.

With difficulty Rosalind tore her eyes away from the fluid ripple of his thighs and met his gaze, suddenly understanding the reason for his total lack of shyness.

He wasn't quite awake, she realised as he blinked lazily at her, his naked arms sliding around her waist as he bent his head to seek a leisurely kiss. His eyes still had that distant, dream-dark look and his mouth was tenderly whimsical as it nuzzled her startled lips apart. His eyelids fluttered shut again. Aside from the rigid thrust of masculinity nudging against her thighs he was utterly relaxed, and his warm body seemed to envelop hers like a butter-soft glove, absorbing her into his languorous dream-world.

'Touch me,' he invited, his tongue slipping inside her mouth and rubbing sensuously against hers. 'Everywhere, all over; I need to feel you all over me...wanting me...loving me...'

His flat hand slid up and down her silk-covered back, massaging her against his chest, his other hand finding hers and drawing it down between their bodies, pushing her fingers into the soft nest of hair. He groaned, racked by shudders as he curled her pliant fingers firmly around him, shaping her to his need, arching his back as he thrust graphically into her soft grasp. 'Oh, God, yes...like that...you know I love it when you touch me like that...'

Rosalind went liquid with pleasure. Luke might have gone to bed wanting to hate her but he obviously hadn't succeeded. She must have disturbed him in the middle of an intensely erotic dream—a dream about *her*...

In Luke's subconscious they were already lovers and now, if she didn't stop him, he was going to turn that dream into reality.

But she didn't want to stop him. She had forgotten the computer disk lying half-hidden under the bed. She no longer cared why she had come, only that she was here and that Luke, in his half-waking state, was open to her in a way he had never been before, expressing his deepest, most intimate needs with a frankness that was usually censored by his extreme reserve.

He was strong in his desire, yet vulnerable in a way that moved her to the depths of her being. Tenderness mingled with passion and she felt a surge of the old recklessness. In his dream Luke spoke of loving, not sex. In his dream he needed her, trusted her, believed that she would never disappoint him...

Rosalind wanted to share his dream. For however brief a time she too wanted to be free of the shackles of doubt, free to need and to trust and believe that love could conquer all. Whatever unwelcome knowledge lurked ahead, at least she could make of this consummation an untainted memory to hold in her heart...

Her hand moved on him and he moaned excitingly into her mouth. She eased their bodies closer together, the slow rotation of her hips replacing her stroking fingers as she caressed her hand back up his chest and over the strong column of his throat, sliding her arms over his shoulders and going on tiptoe to deepen the long, voluptuous kiss.

Her passionate response snapped him to full awareness. His mouth stilled and his eyes flew open, his hands pausing in their restless exploration, one splayed between her shoulderblades, the other shaped to the base of her spine.

His mouth lifted far enough for him to murmur a surprised question that wasn't really a question. 'Roz...?'

'Who else?' She pulled his head back down and flicked her tongue along his parted lips, savouring his delicious surprise as he struggled to comprehend that the woman he held was not the armful of dreams he had confidently embraced.

His gush of breath was warm and spicy, filling her senses with delight. 'I— What...what are you doing here?'

'Making love to you,' she vowed, tilting her head back so that she could see his face. Dark colour ran up under his skin, and his eyes flamed with a scorching hunger as his lips moved soundlessly.

'No...' She pressed a thumb to the soft curve of his lower lip, stilling the formation of another question. 'It doesn't matter how, or why...'

Confusion swirled in the smouldering heat of his gaze. 'But—earlier—you said—'

'Do you want to talk, or make love?' She cut him off huskily, impatient for the violent pleasure she knew he would give her, not wanting her gloriously reckless mood dissipated by cautious reminders.

His teeth nipped at her thumb, his mouth closing over it to suckle it briefly before releasing the moistened tip. 'Can't we do both?'

She shook her head, her rich voice mellowing to a slow, sexy drawl. 'I don't feel civilised enough for conversation. I tend to go a little wild when you touch me and tonight I want to let go completely; I want to set the wildness free. I only hope that you don't find me too uninhibited for your tastes...'

A pulse jolted in his left temple. 'I don't know what my tastes are,' he reminded her roughly, his lower hand unconsciously dragging her hips possessively against him. 'I know so little about women and their physical needs that it's far more likely that *you'll* be the one who's disappointed by my inexperienced performance...'

She cupped her hands over his slightly roughened jaw and slid them down his throat, feeling the ripple of nervous tension as he swallowed.

'This isn't an audition, Luke,' she chided him softly. 'Believe me, you have all the right instincts and that's all that matters. All you have to do is enjoy yourself and the rest will happen naturally.' Her eyes were very green as she assured him gravely, 'And just for the record it's been a long time for me too. Years... I guess I was waiting for a very special man to make *me* feel special... and that man is you, Luke...'

She kissed him and for a moment he was passive, but only for a moment. Then the power of her words shuddered through him and he tipped her head back with the devouring force of his hunger. He held her suffocatingly tight, kissing her with a savage eagerness that shattered the last boundaries of his restraint. His hands relentlessly explored her slender back, massaging lower and lower until the floaty hem of her dress was hiked up the back of her thighs, then sliding underneath to cup her lace-covered bottom, lifting her higher into his groin.

He pulled back, frowning as he watched the silk of her bodice peel off his chest and settle back over her taut breasts.

'I'm naked,' he said thickly, as if he had only just realised the fact.

'I know.' Rosalind playfully ran her fingertips across his shoulders and chest, sweeping them down his sides to linger on the tapered leanness of his muscled flanks. 'I'm glad you don't wear pyjamas. You're very beautiful in the nude; just looking at you excites me...'

His flush deepened and his nostrils flared. 'I usually wear boxers in bed,' he said vaguely, 'but tonight I couldn't—I didn't want anything next to my skin...'

The smile she gave him was sultry and knowing. She dropped her gaze to the point where their hips were sealed together, the erotic pressure preserving his modesty.

'Except me?'

'Except you,' he admitted heatedly, his expression becoming dark and devilish as he watched her smile curve with a hint of complacency, the feminine version of a flung-down gauntlet.

The male in him bristled at her confidence even as he exulted in a fierce sense of victory. The element of danger only added spice to the situation. Edgy, emotional, elegantly sensuous Roz Marlow had finally succeeded in luring herself into his net. Just when he had almost conceded defeat she turned around and did something like this. She was a riddle, wrapped inside a mystery.

But not for much longer. A night of unbridled passion might be all she thought she was offering, but he intended to take more... much more. He would unwrap her secrets just as surely as he intended to unwrap that dainty, delectable body.

His fingers moved provocatively, sliding down inside her fragile lace panties to smooth over the softly rounded cheeks of her bottom. Rosalind shivered and instinctively moved her hips into his touch, but instead of lingering to enjoy her acquiescence Luke continued to plunge his hands downwards, pushing her panties to her knees and then, with a sudden dip and a sideways twist, raking them roughly to her ankles.

He straightened, meeting her startled eyes with a look of blazing male triumph at his reckless daring. To her astonishment she felt herself blush and he gloated openly at the betraying crack in her façade of worldly sophistication. His hands settled firmly back on her waist, holding her steady as he ordered gruffly, 'Step out of them.'

Rosalind obeyed, her legs brushing against his, trembling slightly in response to his smouldering aura of suppressed sexual excitement. He liked giving her orders and her meek show of obedience was an incitement to his boldness.

'Are you wearing a bra?' he demanded in a low, smoky growl.

Rosalind nodded, even though they both knew an answer was unnecessary. He had traced the outline of it while he had been kissing her, his fingers meticulously investigating the seams and identifying the fastening between her shoulderblades. He had merely asked so as to tantalise her with the knowledge of what he was going to do next. He wanted her naked under the liquid silk dress, dressed yet undressed, vulnerable to his desire...

'It's strapless,' she told him unsteadily as his hand slipped through the wide armhole of her halter-necked dress to deal with the hooks. He took so long that she wanted to scream but the combination of taunting deliberation and fumbling difficulty was so much a part of the intensely erotic scenario that Rosalind forced herself to stand still until finally the flimsy undergarment gave way. He tugged and gravity obliged as her bra slithered out from under the loose A-line dress, landing with a hushed thud at her feet that seemed to quake through every nerve cell in her body.

Rosalind had never been so aware of her own sexuality as she was at that moment—never been more anxious for a man's approval.

Luke stared at the polished silk rippling over her skin like a midnight-blue waterfall, a provocative veil for the supple contours beneath. The thin sheen of the fabric was sculpted taut between her high breasts, her nipples jutting out as stiff peaks from which the graceful cut of the dress cascaded away to shimmer and swirl around her slender hips and honey-smooth legs. His chest rose and fell unevenly, his hands flexing violently at his sides, his manhood stirring and thickening against his flat belly. She had been mistaken in thinking that he had been fully aroused when he'd got out of bed, Rosalind realised with a flutter of apprehension.

She had the feeling that in his lovemaking, as in most other things, Luke was capable of a fierce concentration that brooked no distractions. She didn't think he would actually force her, but the familiar vague-eyed absorption with which he was studying her made her wonder if he might unintentionally hurt her in the throes of passion. Yet, oddly, her fear—of his size and the more nebulous threat of his identity—merely gave her own desire an added piquancy.

'Is this what happened in your dream?' she challenged, feeling a slow wave of heat wash through her body at the thought of being compelled to accommodate that potent hardness.

In answer he reached out and cupped her breasts through the silk, lifting the soft mounds and smoothing the fabric with his thumbs so that her distended nipples were outlined even more explicitly.

'This is much better than a dream,' he muttered as her breasts ripened and grew heavy in his cradling hands. He licked his lips and Rosalind unconsciously arched her back but he ignored the subtle invitation. His gaze lowered to her hem and his hands followed, gathering the flimsy fabric and slowly pushing it up her honey-coloured thighs until he exposed a tantalising glimpse of fiery red curls.

'Much better...' he whispered hoarsely, letting the dress fall again, veiling her femininity in a dark swirl of silk. His hands moved up over her belly, shaping the delicate imprint of her navel...up to her breasts again, and back down to toy with her hem...to slip his hand up underneath and delicately brush his fingertips over the unseen fleece...to reach around and massage the silk over the flare of her hips, tracing it into the sensitive crease between her quivering buttocks.

He was playing with her. This gorgeous, naked, *inexperienced* man was playing her like a master...drawing out the exquisite agony of desire until Rosalind thought she was going to explode with frustration at her passive role.

'Aren't you going to take it off?' she blurted out jerkily as he wound a swathe of silk around his fist, forming another shimmering perspective of her body. Luke's erotic absorption faltered and suddenly it occurred to her that perhaps he wasn't quite sure of his next move. 'Or would you like to watch me do it?' she said, reaching behind her neck and releasing the jewelled clasp that was the dress's only fastening.

'Yes, you do it,' he murmured thickly, his hard body glossy with a faint mist of perspiration as he watched her cross her arms and whisk the flared hemline up over her head.

She didn't get any further. Even before she had freed herself from the billowing silk Luke had swept Rosalind backwards onto the bed with a hoarse sound of inarticulate need. Blindfolded in midnight-blue, she found herself pulled beneath him, his mouth and hands eagerly roaming over her desperately squirming body.

He bit into her tender flesh, his groans and whispers of raw pleasure inflaming her smothered senses as he hungrily sought her swollen breasts and suckled fiercely on the engorged nipples while she struggled to free herself from the fabric surrounding her head and arms, succeeding only in entangling herself further. Her frantic writhing and gasps of helpless delight excited Luke to a frenzy and the full weight of his tightly compact body surged on top of her, his hands tugging at her thighs, prising them roughly apart, a groan tearing its way out of his chest as he settled himself heavily into the enticing wedge, his congested loins straining against her fiery heart, probing for its moist centre.

Rosalind finally managed to wrench the maddening dress over her head and toss it aside, but Luke was already rising above her on his arms, his chest rigid, his muscles bunching convulsively as he arched his back and threw his head back, blindly driving himself between her thighs with a guttural shout of gratification.

Rosalind echoed his cry, clutching his slippery, straining back as he sheathed himself to the hilt in her wet warmth. She barely had time to adjust to the agonising pleasure of being invaded and stretched to the brink of bursting before Luke was drawing back with a harsh moan and heaving convulsively forward again in a second, massively powerful thrust, his face contorting in a mask of pure ecstasy as he stiffened and then began to shudder in a violent spasm of completion that left him slumped heavily on top of her. She lay blinking over his lax shoulder at the panelled ceiling, stunned by the speed and intensity of his climax. She could feel him still pulsing hotly inside her tense body.

He shuddered again—a deep, sobbing breath. 'I'm sorry... Oh, God, Roz, I'm sorry...'

He withdrew before she could stop him and rolled onto his back, his chest heaving, his arm thrown across his eyes as he continued the choked litany of apologies. 'Couldn't help it... like some crass adolescent...'

'Luke... *Luke*!' She stroked his up-raised arm. 'It's all right—'

He jerked away from her touch. 'There's no need to pretend, damn it! I told you you might be disappointed.'

He sounded like a sulky boy. She wanted to peek under his arm but the grim line of his mouth warned her not to try. She raised herself on one elbow, her aching frustration turning to indulgent amusement mixed with heady anticipation. 'Are you kidding? For goodness' sake, Luke, I'm *flattered* that you exploded all over me like a firecracker.'

His chest stilled and the arm over his eyes tensed. 'A crazed sex maniac, more like.'

Her heart gave a little flip. 'I prefer to think of you more as a satyr... the combination of that Greek-god body and those eyebrows—well... you're bound to be

governed by your earthy passions when you finally catch
the nymph of your dreams!'

She could see the glitter of his eyes as his arm shifted
slightly. She stretched her supple body and, when she
was quite sure he was watching, casually turned her back
and slid off the bed, bending to pick up her silk dress
and slithering it over her head.

His arm whipped down as he pushed himself up
against the disordered pillows. 'What are you doing? Are
you leaving?'

She smiled at his mixture of outrage and anxiety as
she strolled provocatively back to the bed and crawled
onto it on her hands and knees. 'Certainly not. Now it's
my turn.'

'Your turn?' he asked warily, watching her prowl
across the rumpled sheets towards him.

'To explode all over *you*...' She daintily lifted a slender
leg across his body and settled herself firmly astride his
hips, modestly smoothing her silk dress down over his
tight flanks, intrigued to note the visible ripple that un-
dulated the length of his body. She squirmed herself
slowly into a more comfortable position and lifted a
haughty eyebrow at him as she felt the subtle male shift
between her thighs.

A shadow of a smile quivered at the corner of his sexily
narrow mouth. She wanted to kiss it but instead she
leaned forward, folding her forearms provocatively
across his collar-bone, making sure the unfastened
neckline of her dress gaped to show him her softly
swaying breasts, the erect tips almost touching his chest.

'The first time was for you...this is for me...' She
looked at him through veiled lashes. 'Then it'll be your
turn again,' she said, and laughed at the molten look he
gave her. 'That's how it works, you see...it's called give
and take...a very fertile ground for improvisation...'

His hunger congealed into shock. 'My God, I didn't
even use a condom! Are you using anything?'

'No, but it's OK—'

He twisted his torso to fumble for the soft leather shaving case on the table beside the bed. 'No, it's *not* OK! I promised to protect you and I let us both down. It's *never* OK to leave these things to chance.'

He was so savagely upset by his lapse that it seemed natural to tell him, 'It is for me—*always*—that is, if it's pregnancy you're worried about,' she said quietly. 'My attack of pelvic disease left me permanently sterile. As for the other kind of protection... we both have that safety zone of celibacy, don't we...?'

'Oh, *Roz*...' He collapsed back on the pillows, his hands moving to cradle the classic oval of her face, his dark eyes filled with shocked regret. 'Oh, Roz...'

She shook her head, his unspoken sympathy sinking like music on her heart. 'I've got a big extended family, lots of money and an extremely challenging, fulfilling career. I can't expect to have all that and heaven too! Shakespeare had it right—"what's past help/Should be past grief".' She nipped at his fingers and gave him her famous jaunty, gamine grin. 'And it does mean that I get to enjoy my sexy satyr in his raw, natural state.'

She wiggled her bottom and felt a fillip of joy when he instantly attuned himself to her mood and gave a mock growl, making wicked play with the eyebrows that so obviously enchanted her.

The second time they made love was far more shattering than the first. This time Luke kept careful pace with her, exercising a fierce self-control as she rode his iron-hard body to the pinnacle of bliss, withholding his own bucking release until he could use it to drive her over the edge into a wild, free-falling rapture of the senses.

He proved unquenchable in both curiosity and desire, his stamina equalled by his eager inventiveness, and by the time Rosalind fell asleep, curled against his gloriously sated body, she knew that she had found a precious gift.

When the telephone first rang she moaned, and tried to burrow deeper into warm, musky skin, but eventually the irritating intrusion into her cosy world became too much and she reached out to rake the receiver under the sheet, grunting sleepily into the mouthpiece.

'Luke? It's Jordan,' a terse, static-ridden voice rapped out. 'I just wanted to tell you that you don't have to keep an eye on Roz any more.'

A frown wrinkled her lightly tanned brow. 'Jordan? Jordan Pendragon—is that you?'

There was a small silence. 'Roz?'

'*Jordan?*' She was fully awake now, wriggling out from under Luke's heavy arm, meeting a gaze that sprang from sensuous approval to shrewd alertness as Luke registered the name on her lips. 'Jordan, what's going on?'

'You're five hours behind us . . . isn't this rather early for you to be answering Luke's phone?' he countered curiously.

'Maybe he's keeping a better eye on me than you thought,' she said bitingly. 'Would you mind answering my question?'

Thousands of kilometres away Jordan sighed. 'Now, Roz, you know how worried Olivia was about this letter business. All I did was ask a friend to discreetly watch over you—'

'A *friend*?' she repeated ominously, sharply slapping Luke's hand away as he tried to remove the telephone from her ear.

'Well, he and I knew each other quite well when I worked for the Corporation. He was the colleague I saw when you and I were at the airport. When I went over to say hello and found out that he was going to Tioman, well . . . I know what a straight-up guy he is—not street-smart but physically a tough cookie with a cautious brain that makes him cool-headed in a crisis—I'd trust his judgement of people any day of the week...so I told him about your stalking letters and how you refused to countenance protection and asked if he would mind keeping tabs on my favourite sister-in-law without making it too obvious what he was doing—'

'Well, he certainly stuck to orders on that one,' Rosalind grated, ignoring the blatant soft soap since she was Jordan's one and *only* sister-in-law. Her eyes were chips of emerald ice as they froze on the culprit's grim but unrepentant face. 'And now you've decided your *friend* isn't up to the job of minder after all?'

Tension crackled down the line. 'No, it's just not necessary any longer. I was going to ring you after I spoke to Luke.

'Roz, they've found your letter writer; they've found Peter...'

# CHAPTER NINE

ROSALIND went clammy, an ugly premonition crawling across her skin.

'*They?*'

'The police. He's dead, Roz. He killed himself at his flat in Wellington a few weeks ago...but he was such an unsociable type that they only found the body yesterday. Peter Noble was his name. He took some sort of overdose on prescription medication, poor sod—they're not sure whether it was deliberate or not, because there wasn't any suicide note...'

Roz was vaguely aware of Jordan explaining the pitiful circumstances, and the fan paraphernalia, diaries and letters which led the police to approach the Marlows with their information.

Thank God they had nothing to connect Peter with Peggy through her, she thought, but she was sickened to realise that the police had dated his death at just days before that fateful meeting in the Wellington hotel. That might explain Peggy's mentally disorganised behaviour that day. Had she known Peter was dead—was that what she had been trying so hard to warn Rosalind through the pain of her heart attack?

Perhaps she had somehow got into Peter's flat and discovered his body, but had panicked at the prospect of reporting it, even anonymously. She might have been afraid to admit it to Rosalind, too—hence the elaborate, rambling lead-up. She would have been crazed with guilt and grief.

And ever since, all the time that Peggy had been lying unconscious in hospital, her son had been lying dead in his pathetic shrine to yet another woman from whom he had received nothing but rejection ...

'Oh, God!' Rosalind curled over on herself on the bed, the morning sickness she'd thought she had beaten burning like acid in her throat.

'Rosalind, what is it? What's happened?'

Luke caught the telephone as it dropped from her suddenly nerveless grasp, his eyes on her white face as he lifted it, and after a short, staccato burst of speech conversed quietly with Jordan for several minutes. When he finally disconnected the call his face was as pale as Rosalind's.

'Roz—' He touched her bowed back tentatively, as if he expected her to lash out at him, but she was too caught up in the vivid horror she had created in her mind to resist as he put his arms around her and lifted her curled-up body gently into his lap, his hand cupping the back of her skull, his fingers ruffling her cropped locks as he held her against his naked chest.

'I was right to feel sorry for him, wasn't I?' she whispered, swamped by a fresh wave of guilt. 'But I don't feel sorry now; I just feel ... *relieved*. Part of me is *glad* that he's dead, because that solves my petty little problem!' She hitched a half-sob into his strong shoulder, turning her face into the familiar musky scent of his skin. 'Oh, God, Luke, what if it *was* deliberate? What if he did it because of *me* ...?'

'Shh, don't torture yourself about it,' Luke murmured, bending his head to brush his lips against her clammy forehead. 'You can't hold yourself responsible for the actions of a mentally disturbed stranger. Jordan said that he had a long history of psychiatric problems.'

'But if I'd looked on his letters as a cry for help—'

'Noble apparently had plenty of help over the years. He'd got very cunning at manipulating himself out of official programmes. You were *his* victim, Roz, not the other way around. He didn't even see you as a person.

He didn't want you to know who he was because then he might have been forced to face the reality that he wasn't part of your life and never would be.

'He probably enjoyed the sense of power over you that his anonymity gave him and Jordan said that the police psychologist thought the things they found in his flat indicated a classic pattern of escalation. Sooner or later he would have felt the compulsion to act out his fantasies, and when he found that reality didn't match up he would have resorted to violence to punish whoever had disappointed his craving. If he hadn't been able to get access to you, he would probably have forced some other woman to act out your role...'

He dismissed each of Rosalind's hectic ifs and buts with the same calm logic and then, when her initial shock had passed and she broke into a storm of weeping, he held her, rocked her, softly kissing away her tears until the passiveness of grief became the militancy of passion and she made love to him with a wild fervour that blotted out the pain and reaffirmed in the most elemental way her fierce commitment to life, love and the pursuit of happiness. He was gentle, accepting her desperate desire for sensual oblivion, tempering her wildness with his ready responses, allowing her to use him to exorcise her demons.

Afterwards, as she lay tucked in the security of his arms, the perspiration cooling on her skin, she said croakily, the words raw in the swollen tissues of her throat, 'I should be furious with you.'

'Should you?'

He traced the shadows under her tear-puffed eyes with a light finger. The dawn had become day and the room was suffused with sunshine streaming in through the open curtains. They were lying face to face, their bodies still intertwined, and she could see every nuance of his expression. His deep satisfaction was underscored by a new aura of male confidence.

She sighed. 'I *would* be if I had any energy left!'

She felt as weak as a newborn kitten, aware of a pleasant all-over ache mingled with a bitter-sweet sense of melancholy.

'In that case I'd better do my best to maintain your current state of exhaustion,' Luke murmured, with the unique brand of playful gravity that had first confused her into thinking he had no sense of humour. Now her confusion deepened. She was grateful that her absurd suspicions about Luke being a crazed stalker had been squelched, but his feelings and motivations were even more of a mystery than ever.

When she failed to respond with her usual pertness to the subtle sexual banter Luke discarded his muted playfulness, a dark determination entering his gaze as he realised that Rosalind was trying to ease herself away from his disruptive proximity. His arm tightened around her waist, pinning her to the bed, her thigh still sandwiched between his.

'You can't blame Jordan for grabbing the chance to increase the odds on you being safe. Most people are rank opportunists when it comes to protecting their families. People compromise their own personal integrity—take chances—do things for the sake of people they love that under normal circumstances they would consider completely unacceptable.' His voice had hardened perceptibly, his eyes glittering with a restless fervency as he challenged, 'Haven't you ever done something you *knew* was wrong, for reasons that you believed were right?'

Rosalind thought of the time she had masqueraded as Olivia in order to qualify her twin for a portrait commission from the Pendragon Corporation. Olivia had been in a deep depression at the time and Rosalind hadn't even thought twice about perpetrating the fraud in order to promote her sister's stalled career. That Olivia had ended up with Jordan as well as the portrait commission had been sheer chance!

And now, too, there was Peggy Staines. She wasn't family, but she had been in such desperate need that Rosalind had found it impossible to callously turn her back.

'Well, yes—I have...but the ends don't always justify the means,' she said, troubled by his intensity. 'Sometimes the means are too painful, and who's really to judge whether the ends are worthy of the hurt they cause?'

His mouth tightened. 'As far as that goes we all have to make our own moral choices and decisions; ultimately—right or wrong—we have to face the consequences of our actions. All of us would like to believe that there is someone, somewhere, who would make the same sacrifices for us. You're lucky; you obviously have plenty of people on your side. When he asked me to help, Jordan was only thinking of *you*—'

'Oh, I can understand *Jordan's* thinking,' said Rosalind, her hair a brilliant splash against the white pillow as she turned her head to confront him at eye-level. 'But what about *you*? Why on earth should *you* want to get involved? Especially after I'd given you the brush-off at the check-in counter...'

'I was curious about you,' he admitted bluntly, dashing her fond hopes. If he had told her he had fallen in love at first sight—or even second—she might have been willing to forgive him his secrets! 'I knew who you were so I wasn't surprised that you wanted to avoid any curious hangers-on, and when Jordan handed me a legitimate excuse to indulge my curiosity I couldn't resist. Although I wasn't quite sure how to go about the introduction—'

'You could have tried the truth. You could have simply said you were a friend of Jordan's and that he'd asked you to look me up on the trip,' she pointed out sardonically. A curiosity—was that all she'd been to him?

His eyes narrowed at the jab. 'Jordan said that if you knew, or even suspected, that he'd asked me to keep you out of trouble you'd lead me a hectic dance—deliberately try to make it as difficult as possible for me to keep my promise.'

Keep her out of trouble?

Rosalind gritted her teeth at the condescending phrase, but since she would probably have reacted exactly as he'd described she could hardly argue.

She was suddenly diverted by his last words. 'You actually *promised* Jordan that you'd look after me?' Rosalind, of all people, was aware of the importance—and the cost—of keeping rash promises.

One eyebrow flared quizzically at her surprisingly subdued reaction. 'No, I don't make promises if there's a chance I won't be able to keep them.' Damn it, she had to respect him for *that*. 'I simply promised him that I'd do my best.'

Her eyes kindled at the irony. '*You'd* do your best? You didn't have to *do* anything. I practically presented myself to you on a plate!'

'Dropped into my hands like a ripe peach,' he agreed, for the sheer pleasure of annoying her. Rosalind angry was much less mindful of her tongue.

'And boy, did you take advantage of it!' she accused.

She struggled free of his arm and this time he let her go, watching as she sat up and hugged the sheet while she fished around in the bed for her dress. He finally found it for her—a sadly crumpled ball stuffed under the pillows.

'What are you so mad about, Roz?' he said as she snatched it away from him. He watched her silently debate whether to put it straight on, obviously remembering what had happened last time she had worn it without underwear. He sat up, leaning on one strong arm, and goaded, 'Are you afraid I only slept with you as a favour to your brother-in-law...to clip your flirty wings and keep you out of the beds of suspicious strangers?'

Rosalind pinkened with rage. She wasn't going to let him get away with that outrageous lie. 'The hell you did! Jordan's not a pimp and you know damned well I'm not a gullible tramp willing to sleep with any sleaze-bag who shows an interest! The only suspicious stranger around here has been you...and the only *favour* you were doing last night was for *yourself*!'

'And you, I hope,' he said, with an incendiary coolness that made her realise that he had been deliberately baiting her. 'So...I think we've established that you were curious about me too. The fact that it rapidly developed into something more complex was something neither of us could have foreseen. We both got more than we bargained for out of our curiosity, didn't we? I agree, I had a hidden agenda to mine, but *you* were the one making the decisions about where and how far the relationship was going to go—'

'Yes, but they weren't fully *informed* decisions!' she protested, clutching the balled-up dress to her chest to try to ease the tightness of her breathing. He didn't sound like a man gloating over his one-night stand with a minor celebrity. Men who were only after sex talked about complexity and relationships *before* they got the woman into bed, never afterwards...

His eyes narrowed on her white knuckles before moving back up to her defiant face. 'I hope you're not suggesting I seduced you against your will. If anyone was seduced it was definitely *me*. After all, *you* were the one who crept into *my* room last night—'

'Not because I wanted to seduce you,' she protested hotly.

'No?' He smirked sceptically.

'No! Because I wanted to check out your computer files again. Because I thought you might be Peter and I wanted to see if I could find any evidence to prove things either way!' she flung at him.

His smirk turned to shocked outrage. 'You *what*?'

'Well, what was I supposed to think?' she yelled defensively. 'I didn't know you were bosom buddies with my brother-in-law. I didn't know you were playing amateur bodyguard! I was just going to hack into your system to see if there was proof one way or the other—'

'You were going to *mess around* on my *hard disk*?' he howled. He seemed more affronted at the thought of his computer being tampered with than he was at the idea of being suspected as a psychotic stalker of women.

'I brought back the floppy I took,' she said, lifting her dainty chin aggressively. 'I was going to reread it, but I dropped it on the floor in the dark. And then you woke up and...and—'

'And you realised your suspicions were completely unfounded and utterly ridiculous!'

'Well...you took me by surprise and...uh...'

He read between the lines of her inarticulate stammer and swore with startling fluency.

'So you thought I might be dangerous, but you fluttered up to the flame anyway? Damn it, Roz, don't you have *any* sense of self-preservation?' Each sentence worked him into an even quieter fury. 'No wonder Jordan was worried! Do you realise what could have happened?'

'I thought it had,' she reminded him, with a trace of her old insouciance.

He stamped on it grimly. 'You know how strong I am. If I had been your stalker I could have hurt you, abused you in some perverted way to feed my sick obsession, *killed* you even,' he emphasised viciously. He took her by the arms, giving her an urgent little shake. 'You may

act tough but sophistication is no protection against violence. You don't have the strength to fight a man who
thinks he has nothing to lose—'

'P-Peter's dead, for goodness' sake!' she stuttered, her
heart hammering at the fierceness of his reaction.

'You didn't know that last night! Just what the *hell*
were you thinking, to take such a stupid risk?'

'I refuse to answer on the grounds it might incri-
minate me!'

His eyes sharpened. Too late Rosalind remembered
the frighteningly perceptive observation amongst his
diary of notes that she had a habit of resorting to flippancy whenever her emotions were in danger of being
too deeply engaged. It was a self-protective mechanism
that she had used a lot where Luke was concerned.

'Roz?'

His fingers sank deeper into the soft flesh of her upper
arms and she dropped her dress, pushing against his chest
to no avail. Unattended, the sheet across her breasts
sagged, but Luke didn't take his eyes off her face as he
pursued her with silken tenacity.

'Maybe you weren't thinking at all. Maybe you were
operating on pure instinct. Your logic told you not to
trust me until you'd checked me out, but you've never
been guided by logic, have you? You invariably act from
the heart. What was your heart saying to you last night,
Rosalind?'

She shook her head slightly, her eyes flashing like rare
jewels in the streaks of sunlight that lanced through the
room. 'That I was crazy,' she said breathlessly.

'I know the feeling,' he murmured, vagueness suddenly blanking off his expression.

Was that a declaration? An admission? Why did she
feel that she had disappointed him in some way? What
did he expect from her?

'I keep discovering things about you that put a whole
new spin on your character,' she blurted out in frus-

tration. 'How can I trust the real you if I don't know who that is? What *other* secrets have you been keeping from me...?'

'Only one.' His eyes were hooded. 'But it's the most important one. Are you going to ask me to tell you what it is...?' His hands fell away, setting her free, as he lazed back down in the bed, tension evident in every muscle and sinew. Experiencing a strong premonition of danger, Rosalind drew the sheet back up over her breasts in an unconsciously symbolic gesture of concealment. 'You want us to be totally honest about ourselves?'

'Yes... of course I do,' she faltered.

Luke's lowered lashes flickered as he revealed the hook in his tantalising bait. 'Well, if you want to talk secrets, Rosalind, I'm quite willing... as long as it's mutual. Are you ready for that yet, do you think? Are you ready to bare the deepest, darkest, most important secrets of your soul on the strength of a one-night stand?'

Her whole being revolted at his brutal definition of their night together, even though she knew he had used it deliberately to provoke just such a reaction. 'That isn't how it was—'

'No.' He cut her off smoothly. 'I agree. So let's say we're lovers, then. And lovers are supposed to confide in each other, aren't they, Roz? To share their joys, their sorrows, their guilty secrets...'

Rosalind moistened her lips, knowing what was coming next, as he went on with insidious calm, 'So that must mean that you're going to tell me all about you and Peggy Staines and what led up to her having a heart attack in your room. Maybe you're going to tell me the rumours about blackmail were true...?'

Rosalind threw back her head proudly. 'I *wasn't* blackmailing her—'

'Then *she* was blackmailing *you*?'

'*No!*'

'Then what was all the money for?'

'It wasn't as much as the newspapers said—just a few hundred dollars—and it belonged to someone else. I was simply...minding it,' Rosalind said reluctantly. Peter Noble's last and most frighteningly direct gift had been a thick wad of banknotes stuffed in with his letter and she had intended to ask Peggy to return it. Peggy had had it in her hand when the pain had struck and in the ensuing panic the money had been scattered around the room.

'Was it some sort of drug deal gone wrong?'

She glared at him. 'No, of *course* not!'

'Then what?'

She remained silent, folding and refolding the top of the sheet across her chest. Even dead, Peter Noble had the power to create havoc in Peggy's life.

'Still want to keep your secrets, Roz?' Luke taunted softly as the silence stretched.

She swallowed the copper taste of fear. Why was he pressing her like this? Was it just a matter of principle, or did he have some deeper purpose? He must realise his flatly confrontational approach was bound to rankle. It was almost as if he *wanted* her to refuse...

'This one isn't mine to tell. My promises mean as much to me as yours do to you—'

He pounced. 'Who did you promise? Peggy Staines? Does that mean you know something that could be damaging to her or her husband?'

Rosalind looked away. Oh, he was sharp. So very, very sharp. If she wasn't careful, with a little more information he might piece the picture together. In a way she wished he *would* guess the truth and thus relieve her of the burdensome responsibility she had impulsively shouldered. His impartial, analytical brain might see an honourable resolution to her painful dilemma.

'I'm sorry...' Her expressive voice was redolent with weary regret. This was even harder than it had been denying her own family. The Marlow clan would always stand staunch for one of its members. Her family's love and private belief in her was strong enough to endure the slings and arrows of outrageous fortune. But the relationship between her and Luke was still very fragile and new and she might be damaging it beyond repair by demanding that he take her on faith. 'I can't tell you anything else.'

'Not ever?' he asked with equal quietness.

Her heart quivered with a faint pulse of excitement. 'Ever' was a world without end. His question implied a future that she feared to contemplate.

'Not *yet*,' she temporised.

'Soon?'

She looked back at him helplessly. 'I—no—maybe...I don't *know*!' She wrapped her arms about herself and shook her head. 'I just don't know! Can't we let it drop?'

'So you want us to go on as we are, then—no soul-searching confessions on either side...*yet*?' There was a tormented edge to his words, a duality that suggested that in spite of his attempts to persuade her otherwise he too welcomed the reprieve.

'Oh, you're very clever,' she said bitterly, recognising that he had brought her full circle, knowing no more about him than before, whereas he had managed to eke some valuable information out of her.

She flinched at his sudden movement, but he was only reaching for one of her fretting hands, lifting it unexpectedly to his lips.

'Clever enough to accept the wisdom of the Bible when it says that there is a season to everything,' he said, a strange serenity replacing the aggressive curiosity in his eyes as he kissed the underside of her encircled wrist and placed her hand against his warm chest, his rapid heartbeat providing a counterpoint to his slow words. '"A time to every purpose under heaven...a time to keep silence, and a time to speak..."'

' "A time to love, and a time to hate"?' she quoted shakily as he ran his hand caressingly up her arm and cupped her shoulder, gently tugging.

'Is that what you're afraid of, Roz? Do you think I might hate you when you finally unveil your secrets?' he whispered as he drew her inexorably down on top of his outstretched body.

A sudden smile chased the brooding shadows from her eyes and relaxed her supple body. Of course not. Why would he? 'No...' He might love her, though, if she gave him sufficient encouragement.

'Well, then...' Luke reached up to trace the outline of her soft lips. 'Maybe you're right... maybe this is our time for silence... our season for loving.' His fingers stroked up over her temple and threaded into the shimmering red halo of her hair. 'But that other time *will* come for us, Rosalind...' He lifted his head and exerted just enough pressure on the back of her delicate skull to breathe his vow against her lips. 'One day soon we'll have our reckoning...'

It was a promise Rosalind tried hard to forget over the next few days. After calling Jordan later that same evening to reaffirm the details of Peter Noble's death and check that Peggy Staines's condition remained unchanged, she determinedly dismissed the tangled past and uncertain future from her mind. She decided that for the remainder of her holiday she would live in the golden present, storing up emotional treasures, stringing memories like priceless pearls—pure, precious, unique in their joyous lustre.

The long, blazing Tioman days gave way to equally long, blazing nights with Luke. For all his inexperience, he was a wonderful lover, tender yet fierce, hungry for everything that she could offer and disconcertingly eager to experiment, delighting in his ability to sometimes fluster the unshockable Roz Marlow.

Instead of easing with familiarity, their passion strengthened and deepened, and as they lazed away the days Rosalind knew with utter certainty that her instincts hadn't betrayed her. Luke had melted into her heart until he was an indivisible part of it—part of her...

With Luke she could be gregarious and playful or silent and moody or broody and restless and he would simply be...Luke. He taught her to drink vodka without choking and she taught him to dance. He showed her how to tone her body with weights and she taught him how to abuse his with wickedly licentious desserts. He taught her astronomy while she quoted Shakespearian sonnets beneath the stars.

And they talked, not of important things but of the vital trivialities that bound people in intimacy—the foods they liked and music they preferred, the places they had been to and the books they had read as children. Emotions, like the immediate past and future, were a taboo subject, but Rosalind never doubted that, like her, Luke was discovering a part of himself that he hadn't hitherto realised existed.

Once they came upon some young island children playing on an isolated beach and, as Rosalind stood there wondering what Olivia's children would look like, she felt Luke's hand slip warmly into hers and squeeze. She hadn't been conscious of her melancholy expression and she banished it by flinging herself into the children's chasing game, making them giggle and Luke laugh at her mad antics.

She had thought she had finally come to terms with her sterility long ago, but now she knew what her doctor of the time had meant when he'd talked warningly about cycles of acceptance. Loving Luke had made her aware that, no matter how full and contented a life she created for herself, a secret sorrow would always lurk in some hidden corner of her heart. Any man who loved her enough to be faithful would forfeit his only chance of

immortality. She could offer him every-
thing...everything but a child born out of their love.

The days slipped past with ever greater speed but the
end of Rosalind's holiday was still a small eternity away
when the bubble of wonderful unreality abruptly burst.

Rosalind had breezed into Luke's chalet, laden with
new clothes that she had picked out for him from the
hideously expensive hotel boutique, to find him on the
telephone. He had been going through some of his electronic mail when she had left, as he did most after-
noons, and he was still seated in front of his laptop at
the small dining table, his reading glasses dangling from
his hand as he pinched the bridge of his nose between
forefinger and thumb, uttering brief, monosyllabic re-
plies to whoever was on the other end.

Rosalind put down her packages quietly and as Luke
looked up sharply at the crackle of the carrier bags she
was shocked by the greyness of his face. His hand
clenched on the receiver and she hesitantly mimed herself
going out again but he shook his head abruptly, his attention snapping back to the last few words of his call.
After hanging up he sat for a moment, staring into
nothingness, his cheeks hollowed with strain.

'Luke? What's happened? Is something wrong?'

He stood up jerkily, looking at her but not seeing her,
tossing his glasses down on the table with unaccustomed
contempt for the lenses. 'That was my father.'

'Oh,' she said, taken aback by his harshness. Had they
had an argument? 'What did he want?'

She wondered whether the elder Mr James was anything like his adopted son. Had Luke still been young
and impressionable enough to be moulded in his new
father's image?

'Sit down.' She blinked at the order, a little trickle of
coldness running down her spine. 'I've never told you
much about my parents, have I?'

She shook her head as she perched uneasily on the edge of the couch, watching him prowl round the room tidying things that didn't need to be tidied. He hadn't told her anything but the bare fact of his adoption. Thinking it must be an ultra-sensitive subject, she had respected his silence.

'Actually, my adoptive father is related to me, but only by marriage. My mother was his stepsister.'

Rosalind opened her mouth to protest that he had told her he had been orphaned without a family but snapped it shut again as he continued flatly, 'My parents left a hell of a lot of debts when they died—my father had just mortgaged everything to go into business. His only legacy to me was his name; that was why I kept it when my aunt and uncle adopted me. They couldn't have any children themselves and I've always felt I disappointed them by not taking on their name, but I just couldn't bring myself to reject my last link with Mum and Dad.

'They certainly loved me as if I was their own and I never lacked security, financial or otherwise, and although they demanded strict standards of behaviour of me I knew it was no more than they expected of themselves. When I was at school they never missed a sports day or a play, and they always welcomed my friends. They bought me the best education money could buy and gave me all the support I ever needed in my studies...'

Rosalind sat there listening to him describe how wonderful his adoptive parents were and how much he owed them, gradually feeling colder and colder until her core was solid ice—numb and blessedly unfeeling. He still hadn't mentioned any names, but as he rambled jerkily on she knew... she *knew* ... with a black fatalism that made her wonder if she'd *always* known...

'It's Peggy, isn't it?' she uttered through white lips, when she could stand the torture no longer. 'Donald and Peggy Staines are your uncle and aunt...'

He swung around, knocking one of her packages over, and out spilled a green silk shirt she had bought him because it was the colour of her eyes and she'd thought it would remind him of her when she wasn't around.

'She regained consciousness yesterday morning. Don didn't ring me until now because her condition hadn't stabilised, but now they've had time to make an assessment... The stroke has affected the movement down her left side and distorted her speech but she can make herself understood.'

Peggy was awake and starting to communicate! Rosalind could hardly take it in. She felt as if *she* was having a heart attack, the squeezing in her chest almost too much to bear. She looked up at the towering figure... at the adoptive half-brother of Peter Noble. Poor Peggy—she had had two sons and neither bore her name! She had been forced to give up her first-born child for adoption, who, it had turned out, was destined to be her *only* born, and then through a tragedy she had gained another son, whom she herself had adopted. Luke's love and respect for Peggy bordered on reverence. What would it do to him to learn that she had been too ashamed to appeal to him for help?

'It wasn't just an incredible coincidence that you were on that Tioman flight, was it?' she whispered. 'Somehow you found out and you *were* following me.'

'Don begged me to find out what kind of trouble Peggy was in. He wanted to know if he ought to resign before the scandal breaks. He's that kind of man—painfully honourable,' Luke said grimly. 'He couldn't remember anything of what you'd said at the hospital, only that you'd been vague and evasive, and you'd disappeared pretty sharply. He couldn't leave Peggy so I said I'd track you down and find out what he needed to know.

'Don's police connections were of the opinion that you were certainly hiding something, but they had nothing to work on and they suspected you would bolt at the first sign of pressure, so I put some feelers out at Pendragon before I flew up to Auckland and, thanks to my security rating, I found out about Jordan's extremely confidential travel booking...non-tax deductable.' The typically meticulous addition was made totally without humour. 'I knew the best chance I had to persuade you to help me was to be on that plane.'

Rosalind massaged her aching chest. 'But—I can't believe that Jordan—'

He cut her off with an impatient shrug. 'Our friendship was largely confined to the Pendragon offices; he has no idea who my parents are. Seeing him at the airport—now that *was* pure coincidence. And a profound piece of luck for me. But unfortunately he couldn't tell me anything more than the police, so I knew then that if you weren't even talking to the people you trusted most you certainly weren't going to open up to me. Given what you were being accused of, I didn't think compassion would be one of your strong points. I was wrong about that, wasn't I?'

His sober question threw her off balance for a moment but she quickly regained it. 'Did you think you might have a better chance conning me into some pillow talk?' she flung at him bitterly.

His eyes narrowed. 'It occurred to me—especially considering your royal reputation for reckless behaviour.'

She went white, leaping to her feet, her hand itching to hit him. 'You *bastard*!'

He was equally pale. 'I told you how much Peggy and Don mean to me—'

'And that excuses what you did? I suppose you're going to say the ends justified the means!' she spat furiously. 'And how proud of you would your parents feel now, knowing that you prostituted yourself with a little slut for nothing?'

His complexion flooded with brilliant colour. 'I said it *occurred* to me, that's all,' he said roughly. 'Damn it,

Roz, I'm trying to be as honest as I can with you, for *both* our sakes. I didn't know you back then. I do now...probably better than you would like me to. You know damned well I *made love* to you because it seemed the utterly natural thing to do. There was no ulterior motive, except maybe to build an intimate bond between us that was strong enough to survive whatever truths we had to tell each other.

'And it is, isn't it, Rosalind? Yes, we're angry with each other, and yes, you're feeling frustrated and hurt, and so am I, and yes, *yes*, I'm going to use every argument in the book to get you to tell me what I need to know, but whether you do or not *this is not over*...I won't *let* it be...'

Rosalind had had plenty of flamboyant rows in her time, but never one in which she had felt the pain of the attacker as acutely as her own defensive wounds. On the ferry to Singapore the next morning, clutching only her small overnight bag, she shakily congratulated herself for withstanding Luke's powerful assault on her conscience, on her see-sawing emotions and...finally...on her body. They had made love all night long with a fierce, bruising urgency that should have left her feeling fragile and vulnerable but instead had left her charged with a furious energy. Luke seemed hell-bent on staking a claim to Rosalind's loyalty, both in bed and out. Well, first she would have to clear the decks of *prior* claims...

She had left him still sleeping and signed an early checkout, arranging for the rest of her luggage to be packed and sent on to her the next day, hoping that her scattered belongings would fool Luke long enough for her to make a clean getaway. Unfortunately, when she got to the tiny airport there wasn't a spare seat until an afternoon flight to Kuala Lumpur, so instead she headed for the wharf and gained a last-minute berth on the high-speed catamaran.

As the twin granite peaks of Tioman receded into the glassy South China Sea Rosalind refused to look back. No regrets, she told herself. She had made her decision; now she had to stick to it.

Don't look back, she told herself half a day later as she boarded a first-class flight from Singapore to Auckland via a couple of long, tiresome stop-overs which had not figured in Jordan's original flight plans. She sat bolt upright as they chased the daylight all the way down the Pacific rim, rehearsing scenarios over and over in her head until she thought she was prepared for every eventuality.

Nearly twenty-seven hours after she had blown a farewell kiss to the sleeping man on a tumbled bed in a faraway paradise she stumbled into the starkly modern clinical ward in the Wellington hospital where Peggy Staines was listed as not receiving visitors and immediately got into a full-blown argument with a tank commander in nurse's drag.

'It's all right, Sister, I know she looks dangerous, but she's with me.'

Rosalind gasped at the mirage hovering before her in a faintly rumpled suit, his hair flopping over his tanned forehead, his eyes almost as bloodshot as hers.

'How did you—?'

'Because I told you—I know you almost as well as you know yourself, Roz Marlow. This is exactly your extravagant style—the hotheaded decision, the dramatic exit, the flamboyant gesture of self-sacrifice! Did you think I didn't know the instant you left the bed? Did you think I didn't immediately pick up the phone and ask Reception to let me know if you checked out? Did you think I couldn't spin a good enough sob story to touch the heart of the woman on the flight-information desk at Singapore?

'You taught me well, Roz—you should have stuck with me then you wouldn't look such a total wreck,' he said

cruelly, his eyes flicking over her jeans and travel-stained
T-shirt topped with her denim jacket. 'I pleaded a family
emergency and got priority-bumped all the way from
Tioman. I understand you took the scenic route...'

Her blood sugar shot sky-high—quite a feat since she
hadn't eaten for a day and a night. 'Why, you—!'

The sergeant major harrumphed. 'Don't disturb her
for too long, Mr James. She needs her rest.'

'Uh, that's very kind of you...' Rosalind was mortified. How could the woman be so caring about someone
who had been so insulting? She flashed her a brilliantly
apologetic smile.

'She's talking about Peggy, Roz,' Luke reproved her
as the nurse trod heavily away.

'Oh.' Her eyes darted to his. 'How is she?' He hadn't
tried to stop her leaving Tioman or entering the hospital, yet he was here lying in wait for her. Was he now
going to show her how futile any cunning attempt to see
his aunt would be?

He took her elbow and turned her down the long cor-
ridor, shortening his stride to match her wobbly steps.
'Well enough to see you.'

She just stopped herself leaning on him. 'You *told* her
I was coming?'

'She's in no condition to take any shocks. Don't
worry,' he said wearily. 'I reassured her that although
we know each other we haven't discussed anything that
happened between you two. She seemed pathetically
relieved.

'She told me that she was horribly embarrassed...that she's been a closet fan of yours for years
and got carried away having recognised you having coffee
at the hotel. She said she followed you up to your room
and got you to ask her in by pretending to be a hospital
employee, and that you kindly let her stay for a drink
and a chat while you got ready for your appointment.
She said she thought Don would be angry with her for

behaving like a teenager and she's sorry that she put you in such an awkward position by making you promise not to tell anyone of her foolishness when she started having pains.

'I didn't mention the extent of the publicity but I did say the press interest had put quite a lot of pressure on your silence, and she said she had no idea that her silliness would get blown so out of proportion or she would never have asked such a thing of you...'

Rosalind's heart sank at the blow. Peggy was scarcely awake yet she was already frantically covering her tracks. She expected them to continue their charade for ever! The story actually sounded quite plausible but it was obvious from Luke's toneless delivery that he knew Rosalind too well to believe that so frivolous a reason was behind her unshakeable show of loyalty.

'That's what she's going to tell Don, anyway, and since they both hold that lying is a sin he'll believe it.' He wiped a hand across his face. 'Problem solved for everyone... as long as it's not going to blow up later in his face...'

Rosalind said nothing. What could she say? She couldn't guarantee that the truth wouldn't eventually leak out; she could only remove herself from the situation to ensure that it didn't come from her. Unless she could persuade Peggy to make a clean breast of it, so that they could *all* begin again with a clean slate...

'I hate it that she has to suffer like this,' he went on savagely. 'She's always seemed so strong... and to see her lying there so... so...'

His voice thickened to a halt as they stopped before a plain swing-door with a square panel of reinforced glass, and he placed his palm against it, blocking out her view of the bed within.

'Luke—' She was shocked to see the glitter of tears in his eyes, the way the skin was stretched taut across his cheekbones and jaw. God, he was hurting, and part of his pain was because of her. By coming here like this was she making things worse for Luke and his family just for the sake of her own selfish needs? 'Luke, I—'

'I know...I know...you want to go in alone,' he said, misunderstanding her inarticulate plea. He released her elbow reluctantly. 'For God's sake, Roz, whatever this is about, please try not to hurt her any more than she already has been. She's going to need every ounce of hope and courage to tackle her recovery.'

There was a hot stinging in her own eyes at the irony of his plea. He didn't know what he was asking. To have any sort of future with Luke she might *have* to force Peggy's hand. And if she did she might very well lose him anyway. 'Of course I won't!'

She turned to go in and felt him touch her shoulder. 'And Roz?'

'What?' She looked back, her chin brushing the back of his hand. Unable to resist, she tilted her head and rubbed her cheek yearningly against it, until he turned his hand over and ran his fingers down the line of her jaw to tap them on her chin.

'I love you,' he said huskily.

'What?' She was hallucinating from lack of sleep. Having a waking dream...

'Never mind. Later. Go on...' He flattened his hand between her shoulderblades and pushed, so that she stumbled forward, instinctively reaching out and bumping open the door. 'I'll be waiting for you...'

A long, slow, painfully intense half-hour later he was true to his word, getting up from a hard wooden chair in the small, sterile waiting room at the end of the hallway as she trudged across the wavering floor towards him.

'Well?'

She closed her dry, gritty eyes, unwilling to face the dream that had become a tangled nightmare of lies.

'I have to go.'

'Go? Go where?' His voice sounded as if it was coming from the end of a long tunnel.

'Home.'

'Home?'

'To Auckland... my apartment... I have an audition to study for...' Damn it, she was going to take that Shakespearian role! she thought, trying to summon her enthusiasm. Peter was gone... no more stalker to distract her stage persona, to paralyse her vocal cords with nameless fears. Her career had taken the place of children in her life; now she would stretch it over the gaping hole left by Luke. She would be the fiercest, most blood-thirstily ambitious, most utterly wretched Lady Macbeth in the history of the Scottish play!

There was a long silence and she opened her eyes, to be confronted with the intense black conflagration in his.

'What happened in there?'

She tried to smile, failed and settled for a shrug. 'Nothing. We talked. It's over—I don't have to feel any more horrible guilt or responsibility on Peggy's behalf... she said she'd been having chest twinges for some time but had put them down to indigestion. As for the rest... well...' She found a wall at her shoulder and leaned gratefully against it. Why did her legs seem not to work? 'It was just as she told you...'

Peggy's struggle with language had reminded her uneasily of those terrible minutes in the hotel room and Rosalind had been no more proof against the agitated pleading of her eyes and the working of her distorted face than she had been on the last occasion.

Peggy was deathly afraid of losing her family and, trapped by her disability, more vulnerable than ever to her deeply rooted feelings of shame. She *had* found Peter's body, after calling in at his flat on the way to the hotel, and, as Rosalind had surmised, had fled in shock and panic. But she was under the impression that she had managed to redeem her wickedness by blurting everything out in the confused moments before she'd finally lost consciousness.

Rosalind had tactfully glossed over the facts, hoping that the poor woman need never know of the true circumstances surrounding the discovery of her son's body. Her grief over his death was muted by a shamed sense of relief and, true to the spirit which had characterised her behaviour all along, Peggy was desperate to have the past swept safely back under the carpet where it belonged.

Rosalind hated it but she had been too exhausted to remember her rehearsed arguments, even if she could have brought herself to unleash them on the fragile bundle of humanity on the bed. She had the feeling that in years to come Peggy would continue to struggle with her conscience and ultimately pay the price of suppressing her unresolved grief.

'And where does that leave us?' Luke broke harshly into her anguished thoughts by placing a hand on the wall beside her head and dipping his face to force her to look at him.

'Us?' She was still an actress, wasn't she? Maybe that was *all* she would ever be as far as Luke was concerned . . . but at least she could be the *best*.

Rosalind summoned all her remaining courage and gave a tinkling laugh. 'Oh, Luke, don't be so *intense*. There is no *us* . . . that was just holiday fever . . . spiced up with intrigue and all our suspicions about each other. It's a shame that it had to end in the way it did, but maybe it was for the best, because we're back in the real world now and I really don't think we have much in common—'

She yelped as he shot out his other hand to slam it against the wall. 'Oh, no, you don't!' he hammered out. 'I didn't chase you halfway across the world to be fobbed off with your flighty-actress routine! I told you before you walked in there that I love you. That *meant* something to you—I could *see* it; stop trying to deny it, damn it— *I love you*!'

'Maybe you *think* you do,' she said desperately, aware of the sick woman hovering like a spectre between them.

Maybe in time, as she got stronger and better able to cope, Peggy would relent, but what if she didn't? Rosalind imagined loving Luke, sharing his life, coming into contact with Peggy and Don, always walking on a knife-edge, aware that one careless word might sow the seeds of destruction in his adoptive parents' marriage. She would stifle. In love, as in everything else, Rosalind was an all-or-nothing person. She would love freely and completely or not at all.

'But you're a realist, Luke; you know that isn't always enough,' she continued. 'We . . . we want such different things from life—'

'Yes—I want you and you want me,' he said bluntly. 'Different, and yet the same. We complement each other, Rosalind, we know that we *fit* together . . . like the two halves of a whole.' His hands bunched into fists on the shiny white wall as he looked down into the carved stillness of her coldly classic features. 'If you want this to be our final reckoning, so be it. Look at me and tell me you feel nothing for me. Convince me. Look into my eyes, damn you, and tell me that you don't love me and never could.'

She lifted tragic green eyes, rage breaking through the marble-like stillness of her façade. 'I don't love you, Luke, and I never could,' she snarled, hating him for forcing her to be brutal.

He drew a breath, and his hands fell heavily to her shoulders. His eyebrows slanted and his mouth quirked.

'And people *pay* to see you do this?' He cocked his head. 'Oh, Roz, I hope nobody ever asks me for my opinion of you as an actress.'

His response was so unexpected that she began to slide down the wall. How could he not believe her? She thought she deserved an Academy award for her performance. 'I don't love you!' she repeated feverishly. 'I really don't!'

He caught her by the waist, preventing her from falling off the crazy tilt of the world. 'We've done things round the wrong way, haven't we, Roz... had the honeymoon before the wedding?'

She held her hands up in a warding-off gesture, only to have them captured and kissed. 'Luke, for God's sake, it wouldn't work—'

'Why not?'

A million reasons... most of them to do with other people, she thought.

'It just wouldn't. I have a career that takes me all over the place and I like to move around—have plenty of excitement going on in my life. You wouldn't like it... you're too conventional... you need to be settled... have a fixed home, family... children...' A light went on in her overloaded brain. 'You'd make a wonderful father; you should have a big, loving family of kids to make up for all you missed in being an only child. I can't even give you *one* child's love...'

She went on to tell him that he hadn't thought it through; she listed all the reasons why he would come to resent her childlessness and announced that she never intended to get married anyway because she didn't see the point if there were no children to protect.

'Fine. We'll just live together for the rest of our lives.'

'Luke!'

He cupped her face tenderly. 'Look, Rosalind, I know what you're doing and it's very kind of you, but you can't protect me from my own emotions. Let *me* bear the responsibility for a change. I *have* thought this through. For the last twenty-four hours I've thought of nothing else. I know damned well that you and my aunt are linked in some way that she doesn't want you to reveal, probably by something that happened in her past, something she's bitterly ashamed of—and, for someone of her generation and religious upbringing, it's probably to do with sex.

'Now, I know that you can't possibly be her daughter but maybe you're her connection to someone else— No!' He pinned her mouth shut with his thumb. 'Let me finish. I'm not going to ask you about it again—I won't *ever* ask you. I don't have to. It's between you and Peggy, not you and me.

'Can't you see that telling you I loved you before you walked into that room was an expression of faith? I will *never* lose faith in you, Roz. I *believe* in you. You're a passionate idealist, a true and honest friend, never venal or self-serving at the expense of others, and because I have that certainty in my heart I can accept everything else on trust...

'I love you for *all* your qualities... for your joy and your stubbornness, your fiery dramatics and your deep humanity—yes... even for your sterility.'

There were tears again in the dark eyes, tears and something else that vanquished her doubts and fatigue—a deep, passionately held commitment to what he was saying.

'The pain that you carry from your past is the part of the compassion you bring to the present. I'd love to heal that pain for you but I know I can't; I can only do as you do for those you love: be there when the hurt is too much to bear alone. There might not be children from our love but—oh, Roz, there'll still be love... so much *love*...'

He leaned his forehead against hers and whispered prayerfully, 'I need you to be there for me too, Roz. Through good and bad, in sickness and in health. That's what this is all about. Trust. If you love me, then *believe* in me. Keep your secrets, and believe that nothing will make me betray our love. Please...'

Rosalind's arms went around him, tight and hard. It had taken magnificent courage for him to say all that, to open himself up so completely before she had uttered a single word of love, and she could feel the shock of it shivering through his entire body.

Trust. Betrayal. Rosalind knew which of the two words she associated with Luke. He was intelligent, resourceful, sensitive and strong and deeply thoughtful... of course she trusted his judgement and the depth of his compassionate understanding. He would never betray those he loved, any more than Rosalind would. In that sense they were two of a kind. There would be difficulties ahead but Rosalind knew that there was no secret that she couldn't share with him, no problem or sorrow they couldn't discuss. For now, she was content to hug the revelation to herself, but she knew that one day soon she would talk to him about Peggy and Peter, and in doing so she would create not a gulf but another bridge of understanding...

'The most important scene in my life and it's being played out in an empty hospital waiting room,' she said in a choked voice. 'I somehow expected a revolving set and maybe a full orchestra and chorus. You're a cheap guy with a proposal, Luke James!'

His head lifted. 'Is that an "I believe"?' he asked rawly, a dark splendour dawning in his eyes at her flippant reply.

She began laughing through her tears. Her dear, darling, cautious Luke wanted the i's dotted and the t's crossed.

'Oh, yes, it's an *I believe*. I love you, Luke James. Now and for always, *I believe*...'

# HARLEQUIN PRESENTS®

## The Marriage Maker
### by
### Robyn Donald

Can a picture from the past bring love to the present?

**Coming next month:**
the third and last story in
Robyn Donald's captivating new trilogy

**#1877 THE FINAL PROPOSAL**
**Jan's Story**

Available in April wherever
Harlequin books are sold.

# Happy Birthday to

*Harlequin Romance*®

## It's party time....
## This year is our
## 40th anniversary!

**Forty years of
bringing you the best
in romance fiction—and
the best just keeps
getting better!**

To celebrate, we're planning
three months of fun, and prizes.

Not to mention, of course,
some fabulous books...

The party starts in **April** with:

## Betty Neels
## Emma Richmond
## Kate Denton
## Barbara McMahon

*Come join the party!*

# HARLEQUIN PRESENTS®

"A prolonged stay in my harem will provide me with a long-awaited opportunity to teach you what being a woman is all about."

Will Bethany pay the price that Crown Prince Razul is demanding—and become his wife?

**Watch for**
**#1875 THE DESERT BRIDE**
**by**
**Lynne Graham**

Available wherever Harlequin books are sold.